Book Description

For countless ages, fairies have existed in human lore as protectors of children, sprinklers of magic dust, and bloomers of flowers. Yeah well, fairies have other jobs, too.

Enter Fecanya, Ordure Engineer at Fey World Maintenance Services. She hates her job. Not that anyone who processes ... "leavings," would, but hey, you wanna trade?

When news of an impending meltdown at a wastewater treatment facility, and a messy war between two gorilla factions (ever seen a gorilla projectile?) arrives at the office, Fecanya must use her many talents to prevent both disasters. But is there a mischievous hidden presence behind this?

With the threat of a city covered in filth of epic proportions, and a jungle at the brink of great ape warfare, it will take more than a visit with her stuffy satyr therapist for Fecanya to prevent a disaster and unmask the hidden enemy, before the "leavings" hit the fan.

Out of Ordure

by Ramón Terrell

To
Alisha
Being an Ordure
Engineer sucks!

ISBN: 978-0-9937236-1-2

Cover painting by Nick Deligaris

Cover design by Nick Deligaris

Book Design by Tal Publishing

Published by
Tal Publishing
Vancouver BC

Ramón Terrell, Publisher

Tal Publishing Trade Paperback Edition 2016
Printed in the USA

Chapter One

Fecanya ran a hand through her short, auburn hair, then took a long draw from her Sweetbark cigarette. She closed her eyes. After several moments of pure smoky ecstasy, she blew a purple cloud out of the corner of her mouth.

The therapist made a sound that was between patient and mildly annoyed. "Must you smoke that in here, Miss Fecanya?" He adjusted his half-moon spectacles halfway down the bridge of his wide nose, and eyed the dissipating cloud with disapproval.

Fecanya smoothed her dress. She narrowed her eyes just enough to convey her sentiment, which at this moment was not being able to care any less than she did about the therapist's discomfort. "It helps." She inhaled another puff.

The therapist sighed, something Fecanya had long grown accustomed to. With those ram horns, and bright blue eyes and close-cut curly hair, she'd nearly laughed the first time he'd made the sound. Now, if she didn't hear him sigh at least twice during their sessions, she wasn't holding up her end of the bargain.

"If you must," came the response. He adjusted his spectacles again, then adjusted his already perfectly straight tie. "Now, if we might get down to business?"

Fecanya blew out another cloud. "Whenever you're ready, Leo." She didn't bother to hide her smirk when he frowned.

"How many sessions have we had thus far, yet you still fail to use my proper name? Leowitriss is not difficult to enunciate." He grabbed one of his custom made pen from the jar and dabbed it on his tongue.

Fecanya bent her hand at the wrist over her heart and widened her eyes. Oh pah-don me for not *enunciating* your name, good therapist, Leowitless."

"Wi ... TRISS!" He strangled his pen harder with each syllable. "And can we *please* get this over with?"

For a therapist, this guy is just too easy. Where the hell did they find him? Fecanya leaned back in her chair and crossed her legs, ankle-to-knee, like any good and proper fairy wouldn't. "Whenever you're ready, Witriss."

Leowitriss ground his teeth as he opened her file. The protruding canines from his upper lip might have been menacing if not for the fact he was about as intimidating as an angry pug.

He found the page and adjusted his spectacles again. After several moments, he cleared his throat.

Fecanya cleared her throat.

Leowitriss glared at her over his glasses, then began to read. "So. Impolite behavior. Refuses to work in a team environment. Less than exuberant attitude on the job. Frequent insults to team members ..."

Fecanya tilted her head from left to right, her mouth downturned as she silently mouthed every word the therapist spoke while he spoke them.

Leowitriss sighed. Again. "Why must you be so difficult, Miss Fecanya. You're a fairy."

"Yeah, sure. And what the hell does being a damn fairy have to do with anything?"

2

"Please, Miss Fecanya! Language!"

Fecanya regarded him with an open-mouthed frown, blinked a couple times, then waved a flamboyant hand at him. "What's with you, anyway? Aren't you people supposed to be more ... I dunno ... outgoing? Sensual? *Masculine?*"

Leowitriss was thunderstruck. "You people? Miss Fecanya!"

"Do you like my name that much, Leo?"

"That is unacceptable!"

"I mean, you're all stuffy and prim. You really need to loosen that tie and at least slouch in your chair a little bit."

"That's enough!"

"I mean, you're a satyr, after all. How in Lilith's Underworld are you ever going to attract a female ..." she looked him over, "or male, whatever your fancy, when you're so damn uptight?"

Leowitriss's mouth bobbed open and closed as he failed to find a response.

Fecanya watched in silent amusement as the stuffy satyr adjusted his spectacles, his tie, ran a hand over his horned head, cleared his throat, and fidgeted in his seat. She decided to add one more piece of charcoal to the fire. "By the way. While we're on that subject, how the hell do two satyrs get-it-on, anyway? I mean, you're not the most flexible bunch, what with those fat furry legs that don't completely straighten ..."

"THAT'S ENOUGH!" Leowitriss slammed a thick hand on his desk, effectively toppling his container of custom made pens.

Fecanya leaned back in her chair and snickered as the therapist snatched the pens up and replaced then in the container.

"How ..." Leowitriss stuttered. "How dare you speak to me such? What is your issue, Miss Fecanya?"

"My issue?" She rolled her eyes.

"You are a fairy of Fey World Maintenance Services. Such unprofessionalism simply will not be tolerated!"

"Will you please ... lighten ... up, Leo." Fecanya took another draw from her cigarette. "I get my job done every day. All the other girls get their work done, everything is in order. What's your deal?"

Leowitriss closed her file and leaned over his desk.

Fecanya grinned and slid her finger up the bridge of her nose.

Hand halfway to his glasses, Leowitriss wrinkled his lips and lowered his hand to the table. "Your unprofessional behavior is intolerable. You make fun of your coworkers, have no respect for anyone, and no one enjoys being around you. Your attitude makes them uncomfortable."

Fecanya snorted. "My *attitude* ... makes them uncomfortable. Well maybe you can find someone else to take over my job and kick me out on my ass ..."

"Language!"

"Yes, Leo. I'm speaking a language. Thanks! Like I was saying, maybe one of them would like to do my job, or you can find someone who's more overjoyed to do it."

The therapist looked at her with sympathy. She wanted to punch him in the face, but everyone knew it took a tough skull to grow horns like that. Punch a satyr, even Mr. Pants-in-my-ass Leowitriss, here, and you're guaranteed a broken hand.

"Miss Fecanya. Your job may not be as glamorous as the others, but it is quite necessary. It helps to make the world beautiful. The world needs Ordure Engineers."

Fecanya held Leo's gaze as she took another pull from her cigarette. After several moments, she blew out a long stream.

"Spare me the fluffy talk, Leo. You know it. I know it. All the girls know it. Polish it up and put a bow on it all you want." She flicked the cigarette into the air and snapped her fingers. The cigarette butt burst into tiny purple sparks. "Spare me the *Ordure Engineer* BS. I'm a Shit Fairy."

4

Chapter Two

Every morning before his predawn jog, Richard got up, brushed his teeth, then used the lavatory before admiring his rippling abs in the mirror. They just weren't as visible after that first meal.

Richard had a reputation to uphold as the fastest jogger in his neighborhood. His struggling neighbors needed a figure of fitness perfection to aspire to, even if they could never be like him.

Out on the dirt trial, he came to the same bend he always did at this time in the morning, and angled himself into it as though he were a motorcycle.

He *was* a motorcycle. A motorcycle on two legs, on two feet, fitted in the best pair of Zikes money could buy. He loved Zikes. Their whole slogan was what his life was all about; "Just Execute." That's what he was. A person who got out and executed life. Took it by the horns and got the job done, one perfect stride at a time.

Richard glanced at his iBerry watch. Perfect heart-rate, already up to eight thousand steps, and at the rate he was at, he'd finish his run with an extra five minutes to spare. Maybe he could knock out an ab workout before showering and heading to the office.

He rounded another corner and had to veer to the left to avoid a woman jogging—or more like "snailing"—her way along the trail with her shaggy golden retriever.

"I hope you clean up after that turd machine!" he yelled over his shoulder as he passed. "Lots of people like to enjoy this place, you know!"

He looked back as he started uphill. The lady was smiling and waving a hand at him, though one finger seemed more prominent than the others. He snorted and looked forward again just as he crested the hill. And slipped in a huge pile of mud that sent his left foot flying out and up.

Time seemed to slow as Richard's foot continued upward. In a tiny compartment in the back of his brain, he had just enough time to marvel at the flexibility of his body as he continued his ascent. His right foot left the ground as his other foot generated the momentum necessary to align his back with the earth.

He looked on in helplessness as a tiny droplet of mud detached from the toe of his shoe and set a direct trajectory for his forehead.

Time sped back to normal, and Richard hit the ground like a sack of brittle firewood. His bones stopped rattling, and his breath came back just enough for him to blow it back out again in wheeze. Richard lay there staring up at the sky. He didn't bother to move when he heard the sound of footsteps coming up the hill.

"I thought jackasses were more surefooted," a woman's voice said.

Richard lifted his head just enough to see a fluffy brown tail swishing back and forth before the dog and its human disappeared over the hill.

He groaned, then shoed a fly away from his face. Another buzzed in his ear, and he slapped the side of his head. "Ow!" More flies came. Many targeting his forehead. "Get away from me you little …"

Richard sat up and groaned at his aching back, then gripped his thigh. "Dammit! I think I pulled a muscle." He carefully straightened his legs and leaned forward to stretch. When he touched the underside of his shoe, his fingers came away with some of that damnable mud.

"Ugh!" Richard went to rub his hand on his shorts when he caught a whiff of something awful. He sniffed a few times, then wrinkled his nose.

He looked at his hands.

Then his eyes slowly turned upward as if he could see his forehead.

Richard's mouth slowly fell agape as the realization set in. "Shit. This is … shit. I've got *shit* on me!"

Richard scrambled around on all fours and slipped again. There was a magnificent "squish," that he tried to ignore, but his brain was already too heavily immersed in horror to be slowed down.

Argh! I need water and a towel! Wild-eyed, he looked around. *My God. This is shit!* He tried to get up again, and his hand slipped in another pile. The hand connected to the wrist on which his sparkling iBerry watch was located. *Ah! My watch!*

The sound of giggling from what must have been the tiniest girl in the world, echoed from the bushes off the side of the trail.

"That's not funny," Richard wailed. "Get me some tissue. Get me a towel. Get me something to clean this off. It's shit!"

The giggling grew more frantic as it retreated farther into the woods. Richard looked down at himself, at his watch, smelling his forehead, and he let out a bellow to shame a horse with menstrual cramps.

*   *   *

"Oh come *on*." Fecanya waggled her fingers in the air, and rotated her hands in an arc, spreading the manure into the soil. "How can all of you be so uptight?"

Bloomara made an irritated sound and ran a hand through her shimmering blue hair. "You made a human trip in a collection of bear leavings, Fecanya." She waved her pale green wand at a clump of petunias, and smiled as the funnel-shaped flowers emerged.

"Bear leavings ..." Fecanya sighed. "It was bear shit, Bloom. How could you not laugh at that sound he made? It was like someone kicked a mastodon in the nads!" She made a cupping hand in the air, then rotated it in a swirling motion, then spread her hands. The deer pellets blanketed across the ground, then absorbed into the soil. "And he had it coming. You saw how rude he was to that lady and her dog."

"You'd *cer*-tainly be an *ex*-pert at rude," Garbita muttered under her breath, waving her gray wand over a collection of plastic cups and candy wrappers. "I'll *neh*-vah understand how humans can love the outdoors, yet sully it so."

"If they didn't, you'd be out of a job," Bloomara replied.

"Says the girl with the laborious job of making flowers bloom," Fecanya said.

"We each have our place," Bloomara said.

"Like I said."

"You're not changing the subject, Fecanya." Garbita's green hair floated about her head as she rotated her twig-like wand and the trash spiraled in the air. With one last twitch of her wrist, the wand made a whisking sound, and the trash burst into an explosion of twinkling glitter. She let go of her wand and it floated in the air, waiting for her to take it up again after she smoothed her green dress made of tightly woven leaves. "I must say that humans are exceptional at creating rubbish. It's just laziness, I tell you. How fah is it from here to the nearest waste paper bausket?"

"How faah is it to thee next waste *pay*pah bausket?"

Garbita growled.

Fecanya snickered.

"Stop it," Bloomara said.

Fecanya rolled her eyes. "Looks like we're about done, here." She waved a hand in the direction they'd come, where the posh jogger was likely sniveling his way home. "I'd say he spread all those *bear leavings,*" she glanced at Bloomara

8

with half lidded eyes, "on the ground enough that I don't need to do it."

"It's still on the trail."

Fecanya sniffed. "Fine." She started toward the road and stopped when she heard Bloomara clear her throat. After a moment of tense silence, she started forward again.

"A-hem."

Garbita chuckled.

Fecanya closed her eyes. "What?" When no answer came, she turned around.

Arms crossed over her chest, Bloomara pointed one of her needle-like fingers to the side.

Fecanya ground her teeth. She didn't need to look. She knew what was over there. She started toward the giant oak the bloom fairy was pointing at.

"I ... hate, big dogs."

Out of Ordure

Chapter Three

If ever there was someone who loved their job, Fecanya was the opposite of that. But then, maybe she was being unreasonable. How many fairies had the delight of cleaning up feces day-in and day-out for as long as it existed?

She side-eyed their supervisor, Bloomara, waving her stupid daddy longleg fingers at tulips and roses. *Must be nice to walk around waving at flowers. She gets bees for helpers. I get dung beetles.*

"Problem, Fecanya?"

"No."

With a gesture from her wand, Garbita lifted a collection of trash into the air and dropped it into a nearby dumpster. "Do you *e*-vah wonder that maybe your attitude is why you have the job you do, Fecanya?"

"Do you ever wonder if anyone finds your voice annoying, Garbage Girl?"

Garbita balled her hands into little fists. "*How* many times must I tell you to stop calling me that?"

"I dunno. Give it another try."

"I ... I should ..."

"You should what, Garbage Girl?" Fecanya pretended to lunge back and forth at her, sticking her chin out. "You gonna smack me one?" She tapped her chin. "Gonna put er right here? Wanna box, Garbage Girl?"

Garbita lifted her wand.

"Oh!" Fecanya said. "So you wanna go *that* way. She bounced her auburn eyebrows.

"That's enough, Fecanya!" Bloomara stepped between them. "This is too far, even for you."

Fecanya lifted her chin. "Tell miss 'perfect garburator' over there to watch her mouth. I didn't start it."

"Your attitude has been worse than usual," Bloomara replied. "Shall I put in a report to increase your weekly sessions?"

Fecanya waved her hands in a warding gesture. "Good grief, no. Look ..." she turned to Garbita. "Look, I'm sorry, alright? I'm in a bad mood, and your remark set me off. Okay?"

Garbita sniffed, and tossed her green hair over her shoulder. "Well, that's fine. *Honestleh*, Fecanya. There's no reason for all this *bo*-thuh. Can we not talk it out like mature fairies? We're in this together, you know."

"Yeah I know. Fairy power and camaraderie and all that. But ..."

Garbita held up a hand. "I know what you're about to say, but it makes no difference. Not every job is prestigious, but every job is necessary." She drew herself up to her full one-foot height. "I may be a Detritus Redistributor—"

"Garbage Fairy." Fecanya took one hand off her hips and waved it in her direction. "Continue."

Garbita glared at her, and cleared her throat. "Yes, well ... just because I redistribute *rubbish* makes me of no less worth than Bloomara or anyone else."

They both looked at Bloomara who quickly unfolded her arms and went to the task of working a clump of flowers that were already flourishing.

Fecanya snarled at the uppity bloom fairy, then looked back to Garbita. "Yeah well, great story. We're all important and everybody gets a certificate of participation with a little trophy. Let's just get this over with and go home."

Garbita looked her over. "*Why* do you choose to dress in such unflattering garb? You have such a ... *love*-ly figure. Surely something with maple leaves. Or even bamboo?"

Fecanya glanced down at her dress, fashioned from a good stout potato sack. "It's functional, and I can wash it a million times and it holds up fine."

Garbita opened her mouth to say more, but Fecanya turned away and went back to her "unsavory" task of "redistributing" the fecal matter of a stray mutt. "Bamboo dress," she muttered. "Why not wear a ballroom gown while I work?"

Ever since she'd been reassigned to Garmon City, the questions had been endless. Why did she wear such boring dresses? Why did she keep her hair so short? Why was she so skinny?

Why are they all so stupid? She ground her teeth. Seriously! Who in their right mind would have long flowing hair in her profession? And a dress of bamboo leaves. Really? So she can soil it at first opportunity when it gently flowed in a breeze to settle ever-so-slightly across a hulking cow patty? And she was willing to bet that if any of those prissy-puss fairies did her job for an hour, much less a day, they'd be just as skinny. Some things you just don't desensitize to, and being an expert at excrement was one of them.

The wand inquiries were the worst. "Why don't you ever use your wand?" Fecanya ground her teeth harder as she stole a glance at Bloomara, waving her simple twig-like wand in the air. She'd just been transferred here at that time, so she'd had to be polite and tell them it was because she liked to stay in practice.

"If you grind your teeth any harder," she heard Bloomara say from farther down the alley, "they're going to throw sparks."

"Oh just bloom your damn weeds," Fecanya snapped.

Bloomara gave her a hard stare, then waved her hand over a small patch of flowers growing through a crack where the wall of a building and the street met.

"Bogey's!" Garbita hissed.

Fecanya quickly snapped her fingers, and the dog dung burst into gray dust that hit the street and sank between the cracks. Her four dragonfly-like wings snapped out and fluttered, and she sped above the ground much like a duck runs just above water.

The three fairies took refuge behind a rusty Gremlin on three flat tires. Fecanya wrinkled her nose. She wanted to flatten the last tire just on principle.

A vehicle that looked much like a massive armadillo with huge, straight tusks, rounded the corner and started into the alley. It gave a loud groan and closed in on the dumpster. As the vehicle neared, the tusks lowered in front of it, and slid neatly into the slots on either side of the dumpster.

A human hopped out of the armadillo-like machine and went around to the back as the tusks lifted the dumpster high over its head and toward the gaping maw in its back. The tusks stopped, and the dumpster bounced in place, then the tusks angled upwards, and the contents puked out of the dumpster and into the waiting maw.

As the tusks brought the dumpster back to the ground, the human at the rear activated some sort of switch, and the giant maw began slowly closing, chewing its meal of garbage. While the maw was mid-mastication, the human went back around front and hopped in the passenger side as the giant metal armadillo began backing out.

The three fairies waited until the groaning vehicle was out of sight before stepping out from behind the back of the Gremlin.

"You see there?" Garbita waggled her fingers in the direction the garbage truck had gone. "That's two honest men doing an honest day's work. Do you know that in human society, those who collect and process rubbish are highly paid and appreciated by many? Human civilization would come to

14

a diseased halt, if not for people like those good men ..." she nearly jumped out of her skin at the sound of loud "POP," and rounded on Fecanya, who was crouched beside the now-flat fourth flat tire on the Gremlin, looking over her shoulder at Garbita with a devious grin on her face.

"Fecanya! *What* is the matter with you?"

She waved a casual hand. "Oh relax. It's not like this car's going anywhere on three flat tires, a rusty chassis, and likely an equally decaying engine."

Farther down the alley, Bloomara was shaking her blue-haired head.

Garbita's mouth worked in silent admonishment as she looked side to side as if searching for the right word.

"You look like a drowning fish, Garbage Girl. Close your mouth."

Garbita closed her mouth with an audible click. "Stop ... calling ... me ... that," she said through clenched teeth.

"I think we're done here," Fecanya pointed down the alley. Can we go? Miss 'pollinate-flowers-out-my-ass' is gonna find more work for us to do if we give her a reason."

Out of Ordure

Chapter Four

Just as Bloomara raised her wand to create the portal back to Fey World Management Services, Garbita called out.

"Ladies! Look at this."

Fecanya and Bloomara looked over their shoulders to see Garbita—or rather, the green bun on top of Garbita's head, as the rest of her was hidden behind a newspaper—slow-walking toward them.

Bloomara put her hands on her hips. "What is it? You know we don't meddle in human affairs, and it's time to punch out for the day."

Fecanya frowned at the supervisor. "Meddle in human affairs?" She waved a hand at the alley. "You help plants bloom so that the bees don't get overworked, thus pissed off, and start stinging humans on sight." She waved a hand at Garbita. "She helps collect garbage and dispose of it, or else Waste Administration's employees would get overwhelmed and probably revolt, or something. I keep the city from flowing ankle deep in—"

Bloomara arched a blue eyebrow.

"*Leavings*," Fecanya said. "Our whole business is meddling in human affairs."

"You know what I mean."

Garbita's head bobbed from behind the giant newspaper. "I know the rules, Bloomara, but this is *in*-teresting." She peeked over the top of the page. "This *should* be interesting to you too, Fecanya."

"Oh?"

Garbita disappeared back behind the paper. "It says here that a certain *Doc*-tor. Carlisle ..."

"Isn't that an actor?"

"... has invented a giant mach*ine* that can more effectively process solid waste."

"Read on," Fecanya said in a husky voice.

"App-*ar*ently, this machine can process at a rate one thousand times *fast*-er than the mach*ines* currently in use at the wastewater treatment plants." She looked up from the paper again, with wide eyes. "And it's twice as big."

Fecanya's pupils dilated. "Twice as big? And it can process a thousand times faster, you say?" Her head fell back, and she blinked slowly, staring up at the beautiful clouds sauntering across the sky.

Images of an enormous treatment plant appeared in her mind. State of the art processing vats converting all of Garmon City's biological unmentionables into fertilizer. Long, beautiful tubes funneling the fertilizer to trucks, who distributed it to soil all over the city and surrounding areas to the endless cheer of vegetation everywhere. Fecanya joined in that cheer. She spread her arms and her little transparent quartet of wings fluttered, lifting her into the air as she turned a slow circle, basking in the endless joy of the constant nourishment of Garmon City's plant population.

And she didn't have to do any of it. All she had to do was order another martini. Or maybe a Bloody Mary, or frozen hurricane with a quarter of the booze. Those things could knock down a full grown human, after all.

Maybe she'd travel the world. Learn a bunch of languages. Eat different kinds of food. Fecanya had a special place in her heart for pastries. Except those twisty glaze donuts. She hated those twisty donuts. Hated them.

The murmur of the ocean caressed her mind. It was like she could hear it gently calling her name, like an audible massage. Fecaaaaanya. Fecaaaaanya. Fecaaaaanya.

"FECANYA!"

Fecanya's eyes snapped open and she lurched sideways in the air and dropped on her rump. She groaned a curse and looked up to see Bloomara staring down at her, arms crossed over her chest, blue eyebrow arched. Next to her, Garbita chuckled.

"Have you taken leave of your wits?" the supervisor demanded.

"Don't get your wings in a wrinkle. What are you talking about?"

"You were floating in the air and turning circles with your eyes closed," Garbita explained. "And you had the most exultant smile on your face."

Fecanya looked around, then over her shoulder at the filthy alley, which had all the appeal of freshly fertilized farmland. She was about to climb to her feet when she heard the faint sound of giggling, echo through he alley. She looked around. "Did anyone hear that?"

Garbita rolled her eyes. "What *are* you talking about Fecanya? The only sound in this alley is coming from us."

Fecanya knew she wasn't going crazy, despite hearing another round of giggling.

Bloomara tapped her foot. "If you're planning to sit there all day, I'm sure Deliah will be happy to approve overtime ..."

"No, no. That won't be necessary." Fecanya hopped to her feet and strode past them. "No need to disturb Lieutenant Commander Hard-Ass."

"What was that?" Bloomara said.

"Nothing. Let's go."

*   *   *

19

Fecanya stepped out of Bloomara's portal and leaned against the wall. It was always a little disorienting when traveling through someone else's portal.

Garbita rested against the wall next to her, similarly trying to reorient herself. "I do wish she'd be more *gra*-dual with transport. The way she just snaps it shut at the end is enough to make me queasy." They both glared at the bloom fairy's back as she stalked away.

"Why would she bother to do that?" Fecanya replied. "Miss second-in-command to Lieutenant Commander Hard-Ass is gracing us with her presence out there."

Despite her prim and properness, Garbita laughed. "Would you like to go for tea?"

Fecanya shook her head. "Nope. I have an appointment that starts just about immediately, and after, that I predict I'll not want to be around another life form for the rest of the day."

Garbita clicked her tongue. "My dear, you *must* try not to be so dour. You're *quite* lovely in a ... truculent, sort of way."

"Way to backhand that compliment, Garbita."

They stood wrapped in dithering silence until Fecanya jabbed her thumb over her shoulder. "Yeah well I gotta ..."

"Oh yes of course. Your appointment. Well. Good day, Fecanya. I suppose I shall see you on the *morrow*."

Fecanya just smiled as the garbage fairy bobbed away. "Of *coouurse*," she placed the tips of her fingers over her heart. "On the *morreuw*."

She turned and stomped away in the opposite direction, secretly hoping that if she stepped hard enough, she might just stomp out whatever feelings approaching friendship she had for Garbita. Truth be told, as much as they argued, it was usually instigated by Fecanya. Not to discount how irritating the hoity-toity fairy was at times, but she couldn't really blame Garbita. She'd spent most of her endless life across the pond, and somehow still hadn't yet emerged from the Victorian age.

"On the morreuw." Fecanya snickered.

She stomped past the Board of Directors room, then turned a corner and stomped down another hallway until she came to the end. She leaned on the guardrail and gazed out at the Rotunda. Despite her mood, the sight of the Rotunda always made Fecanya sigh in appreciation of the architecture.

If there was one thing bees were good for, it was their word. Long before Fecanya had been transferred to this location, the fairies in this region had worked a deal with the local bees. As humans had begun to overpopulate, as was their custom, the bees were becoming overtaxed, and so the fairies had come in and offered to supplement their efforts, in exchange for some of their hive architectural designs.

Exhausted Queen Hilda had been quick to agree, and had her best architects assist the fairies in adapting their designs to create the Rotunda. The huge open space was many stories high and accessible only by flight. At the ground floor, industrious folk from every part of the world worked together like individual parts of a well-oiled machine.

Construction and miner goblins hauled rocks and debris out of the tunnels where the dwarves continuously hacked and shoveled, creating and maintaining the spider-web of tunnels that connected the network of buildings and offices in the sprawling facility.

"Hiya, Fecanya!"

She closed her eyes. "Hello, Sugressa. What brings you to my quiet space, today?"

"Oh don't be such a sour sprout." The chipper sugar fairy practically danced up to lean on the rail beside her.

Fecanya looked at the girl from the corner of her eye. Sugressa was sickeningly bubbly. Always. Her flowing pink hair lay over her shoulder, her "perfect" bangs covering her right eye. Her tiny purple lips stretched into a perfect little smile, and her perfect little purple eyes—well, eye—twinkled with the perfect amount of perfect friendliness. The girl was the embodiment of sweet to the point of disgusting. Cloy.

21

Fecanya forced a toothy smile. She could land a perfect left hook to that perfectly covered right eye, and Sugressa would never see it coming.

Sugressa draped an arm over the rail and leaned over to look down. "Amazing what they've managed to do in so short a time. They just hired clan Heavypants two days ago, and they've already completed sixty tunnels and connected them all! Do dwarves even sleep?"

"They're too cantankerous to sleep," Fecanya said. "They just eat gravel gruel and rock hard dinner rolls in-between shifts."

Sugressa giggled. It was like listening to someone tap a spoon to a glass. You just wanted to snatch the spoon away and shatter the glass, then hand it back.

"Why the long face, Fecanya?" Sugressa asked. "You're such a beautiful fairy, with that lovely styled orange hair of yours, and that beautiful smile you rarely let anyone see. And those green eyes." She poked her bottom lip out. "I wish I had bright eyes like that." She looked Fecanya over and grinned. "And there isn't a single fairy in this entire facility that can rock a potato sack dress like you can. The rest of us would just look like rough brown wedges in it."

Fecanya felt heat rising to her cheeks. "Oh knock it off already. You're gonna make my teeth rot with all that sweetness, Cloy."

Sugressa's shoulders slumped. "Why do you always call me that? I wish you didn't."

Great. Now I'm an ass. She reached her arm out, then snatched it back. After several attempts, she finally gave the sugar fairy a robotic hug, patting her on the back. "Sorry, sweetie. Didn't mean to … you know."

Sugressa sniffed. "Oh I know. It's part of your thing." She looked up. "But a smile here and there would do wonders for you, you know."

You … make … things … sweet, Fecanya thought. *How could you not smile? I'd have nothing but a grin on my face if all I did was sprinkle sugar everywhere. People are happy when there's sugar. They're not so happy in the presence of shit, and neither am I.* "Yeah I'll work on it."

Sugressa straightened. "Good. You should!" Without warning, she wrapped Fecanya in a hug. "I gotta go. There's a pastry competition I'm assisting with. See ya!"

She released Fecanya—who'd groaned in protest through the whole thing—and hopped over the rail, fluttering up and out of sight.

Fecanya shook her head and continued on, allowing herself to enjoy the sight of the endless rows of honeycombed living quarters and private offices that lined the arcing walls of the Rotunda.

A flock of eumenides flapped by, and one broke off and started in her direction.

Fecanya groaned at the impending delay. She may not want to go to her daily session with Leo, but she'd rather just get it done and spend the rest of her day in her room, blissfully alone.

The eumenides flapped on gray bat wings up beside Fecanya and smiled, revealing teeth that belonged in a shark. "Well hi, honey!"

Fecanya forced herself not to shiver like she always did in the presence of the frightening lady. With great leathery bat wings flapping to keep aloft a body with feathered, eagle legs, and a woman's torso, the eumenides was the kindest and most horrifying creature in the facility. "Hey there, Janet. How're things?"

Janet closed her glowing red eyes and casually waved a claw equipped with talons so sharp, Fecanya was sure they could cut her just for thinking about it. "Oh same thing. Just doing my part to help where I may. Donna down at Stardust Processing accidentally inhaled a rather large dose of Sensuality Powder and kept coming on to Joseph."

Fecanya barked out a laugh. "Joseph the gnome that thinks he's a dwarf?" She snorted. "Good luck with that."

Janet chuckled, and Fecanya's mirth froze in her stomach when those shark teeth parted. "I know, girl. I know." She

23

pinched the bridge of her nose as she laughed, and Fecanya had no idea how the eumenides didn't stab her own eye out. "Let me tell you, it took me an hour just to get her under control! She kept trying to drape her wing around him and whisper sweet nothings into his ear."

Fecanya's eyes widened, her fear briefly forgotten. "Oh don't tell me ..."

Janet nodded. "The half-Peacock look."

Fecanya burst into laughter. "What is it about daemons?"

Janet raised her claws and shrugged. "Well at least most daemons can decide on a single form. I haven't seen Donna take on just one form in," she tapped one of those fearsome talons on her scaly cheek, "hmm, about a hundred years, give or take. I actually had to carry her out of the mines while Joseph retreated deeper in and tried to mingle with the miner goblins."

They shared another round of laughter.

"How I wish I could have been there to see that," Fecanya said. "And sadly, I really should be going. I've got an appointment."

Something akin to sympathy glowed in Janet's red eyes. It made Fecanya's soul shiver. "Aw. Honey. I hope it gets better for you. You know we all love you, here."

Doubtful. "Thanks, Janet."

"Think nothing of it, sweetie. You know I'm here to talk if you need me."

"I know, and thanks."

The eumenides waved as she flapped away, her feathery eagle legs tucking in as she ascended. "Feel free to stop by if you want. I'm home all night."

Fecanya waved, having no intention of visiting Janet's lair. "Thanks, girl."

She moved along at a brisk walk. She couldn't afford to be delayed any longer. If she missed even a single session with ole Leowitless, Miss Hard-Ass would have *her* ass.

Chapter Five

She stopped at the door and raised her hand to knock, but hesitated. *How bad would the punishment be if I don't ...*

"Please come in, Miss Fecanya."

She sighed and opened the door.

As always, Leowitriss was sitting behind his desk, filling out some sort of paperwork and humming to himself.

Fecanya remained where she was, not for the first time, looking around at the sterile office. A portrait of Leo with a group of his golf buddies hung on the wall to the right, while his various degrees and certifications hung all about the wall on the left.

Leowitriss looked at her over the top of his spectacles. "Please have a seat, Miss Fecanya. I'll just be a moment."

Fecanya crossed the room and sat down in the chair opposite the therapist. She laced her fingers together on the desk and waited, while he continued to write. After a few minutes, she unclasped her hands and drummed her fingers on the desk, which earned a controlled scowl. *Well then hurry up, you pudgy bastard.*

After a few more minutes, Leowitriss neatly stacked his papers and placed them to one side. He wheeled his chair back and half turned to open the file drawer. Fishing a fat-fingered hand in, he pulled out the thickest file in the row and dropped it on the desk with a heavy thud.

Leowitriss looked down at the massive file, then up at Fecanya.

Fecanya looked down at the massive file, then up at the therapist. After several moments passed, Fecanya asked, "What? You want me to open it?"

"I was hoping perhaps you'd notice the size."

"We're about to add another page to it if you don't get on with it, Leo."

"Your impudence is intolerable."

"Is there anything in that stack of papers that says anything about me not doing my job?"

"That's not the point."

"Is there anything in there that says I'm slacking?"

"You know that's not why your here!"

The satyr's uncharacteristic slip of temper caught Fecanya by surprise. She always irritated him, but this was actual anger. "You gonna be okay, Leo?"

The therapist adjusted his tie and yanked his sweater vest straight. "My name is Leowitriss," he said through clenched teeth.

"You gonna be okay, Leo*witriss*?"

He heaved a great sigh and opened the file. "The past three days, you've caused great frustration to your coworkers. You lit a row of firecrackers between the feet of a human ..."

"He was drunk and pissing on the wall of a store."

"You hid in the shadows of an alley on a Saturday night and magically flung a pile of excrement at the side of a man's head."

"He took a damn *dump* in the alley! It didn't belong there, so I gave it back to him!"

"It is expressly forbidden to use magic on, or interfere with humans."

"Does that mean I'm back on country duty?"

"What?"

"Well that log he left in that alley was his. And he was a human. And since he was human, and I interfered, does that mean I'm back on country fertilizing duty?"

Leowitriss removed his glasses and placed them on the table.

Fecanya watched as the rectangular eyewear slowly descended to the table. Then she looked up into the satyr's beady little blue eyes.

"Miss Fecanya. You are a good fairy. By all accounts, you are an excellent worker, and it is completely understandable that you grow weary of your job from time to time. That's why I'm here."

"And I'm sure some of the other saps around here are in desperate need of your services," Fecanya said. "But I'm not one of them."

"I think if you'll be honest with yourself, you'll see that isn't true."

Instead of another quip, she heaved a great sigh, and looked down at her hands resting in her lap. "Alright." She looked up. "Just ... I've never really opened up about this before, okay?"

"This is a safe space, Miss Fecanya. What you tell me, stays in this room. I'm here to help."

"Yeah well ... I just don't like talking about it." She twiddled her thumbs. "Back out in the country, I was on the farm working the chicken coops while farmer Funkle and his family were asleep."

Leowitriss entwined his three fat fingers and smiled. "Please continue."

"Yeah yeah, right. Well I was working my way to the Afro Chickens ..."

"Afro Chickens?"

"Yes. You know, those chickens with the ..." she waved her hands in a circular motion over her head, "the ones with the neatly manicured feathers on their heads. You've never seen one?"

"I'm afraid not."

27

"Shame. It's amazing how much trouble they go through in keeping them perfect. Except the roosters. They just comb it all over the place and it looks like a feather duster. Anyway, I was working my way there, when I saw a couple of teenage boys hop the fence and creep toward the cows."

Fecanya scowled. "Little shit-kickers were out cow tipping. You know you can kill a sleeping cow when you tip them over? Ya. I wasn't about to let that happen, so I slipped out of the coop and called to a couple of hobgoblins that were cruising the area looking for something to do. I made my way over to the cows and quietly woke them all up and warned them about the incoming bush boys."

"When the boys got close and started to push on one of the cows, she half turned and smacked him in the face with her tail."

Fecanya grinned. "On my signal, the hobgoblins grabbed a bunch of dried out cow patties and started flinging them like Frisbees. You ever see something like that?"

Leowitriss shook his ram-horned head.

"I'll tell you, it's a sight. I used a little magic and guided the "Frisbees;" maybe gave them a little more speed, too. The first one smacked one of the boys in the back of the head so hard it exploded on impact. As he was falling face first in the mud, another one hit his friend in the face. It was like watching two boys being bombarded by unidentified flying cinnamon buns."

"When they finally stumbled to their feet and started running away, I grabbed the hobgoblins and we ran to where a trio of centurion centaurs were waiting. We mounted up, drew our swords, and with a mighty battle cry ..."

"Get *out*."

Giggling, Fecanya bolted out of her chair for the door, slamming it shut half a second before the flying business card holder crashed against it. She had to give ole Witriss some credit; that thing hit the door in the exact same spot every time.

Chapter Six

Mood lifted, Fecanya skipped along the hallways on her way back to the Rotunda. She passed worker gnomes and dwarves grumbling at each other as they shoveled and hacked with their pick axes. She felt sympathy for the smaller gnomes, as working with dwarves was probably one of the hardest jobs one could have. Not only did the walking mini-boulders seem to never sleep, but they weren't very polite, either.

Fecanya made it to the Rotunda and gazed up at the massive beehive replica. She spread her transparent wings and zipped into the air, passing the hundreds of pods and offices that lined the walls in perfect recreation of their tiny six-sided counterparts.

The one bit of luck Fecanya had had when she was first transferred to Garmon City, Arizona was her room. Being that she wasn't as social as most fairies, she'd found a solitary room right at the top of the Rotunda. Not only was it one of the biggest rooms, but it was also encased farther back in the wall. If there was one thing Fecanya valued, it was her privacy.

High above the still-working dwarves on the ground floor, Fecanya waved her hands in front of the dome shaped film that was the door to her room, and it dissolved. Wings still beating to keep her in place, she took a moment to ensure there was no dirt, mud, or any other form of filth about her person, then floated into the room. She half turned and waved a hand back at the entrance, and the tinted dome formed once again.

Fecanya took her time to walk through her beautiful and spacious pod, a smile creeping across her face. She ran her hand along her little marble table and sighed. Old Davin Gravelchin had made it for her several months earlier, when first she'd arrived at Fey World Maintenance Services.

Fecanya went into her wardrobe and donned her favorite pair of cotton, two thousand thread count, two piece jammies, and slippers. She snapped her fingers in the direction of the marble table, and a pitcher of tea appeared and started boiling.

She went to her little library and selected a book, *The Adventures of Super Lady Marmalade*, hopped on her bed, and crossed her legs. Several pages into her book, the teapot whistled. Without looking up, she snapped her fingers, and a little tray and teacup appeared next to her. She made a smooth waving gesture toward the tray, and the pot floated across the room, stopped over it, and filled the little ceramic cup.

Pinky finger straightened, Fecanya lifted the rim to her lips and enjoyed the smooth, lavender tea.

She was just taking her last sip, when she heard an object slide out of the tunnel opening in the ceiling. It landed with barely a sound, and Fecanya looked over the top of her book to see a letter resting ominously on the marble table.

She stared at it without blinking. Only two individuals sent her letters, her marvelous therapist, ole Leowitless, or Lieutenant Commander Hard-Ass herself, Deliah Harmass.

Fecanya continued to stare at the letter across the room. It was a bomb. A bomb waiting to explode bad news all over her the instant she opened it. With a grunt, she snapped her fingers and motioned the letter over. It lifted from the table and shot across the room.

And smacked into her forehead.

Never work magic in your own direction when you're angry. She snatched the envelope off her forehead and opened it. After reading and rereading the contents of the letter, Fecanya flopped back on the bed and stared blankly at the ceiling.

Out of Ordure

Chapter Seven

"Not again."

Fecanya eyed Sugressa. The bubbly fairy was rarely in anything other than an annoyingly chipper mood.

"They can't be at it again."

"You wanna read it?" Fecanya whipped the note out and held it right under the Sugressa's nose, which she wrinkled.

"Um. No. Thank you. I can practically smell the stink in the letter. "Why are these smelly primates always fighting?"

"It's all the processed food and scientific diets," Garbita replied.

"Wrong smelly primate," Fecanya said. She looked around them at Bloomara. "Why do we have to get involved in this at all? I doubt they'll kill each other."

"You already know the answer to that." Bloomara took a sip of her tea, then made a sour expression. She leaned forward and called down the table. "My good dwarf. Might you pass the honey?"

"Might ye pass yer arse down the table and get it yerself?" came the reply. The dwarves laughed.

Fecanya folded in on herself and snickered. When she glanced three seats down and saw that Bloomara had her wand in a white-knuckled grip, she figured she'd better disarm the situation. "Alright come on, Larry. Stop being an elephant's arse and pass the damned bee puke!"

The dwarves—including Larry—laughed all the louder, and slid the pitcher over.

"Ye be sure and tell yer bloomin' friend that the honey's nice and organic." More laughter.

"I don't like getting in the middle of a gorilla conflict," Garbita stated.

Fecanya gave her an innocent look. "Reeaally? Oh but why not, milady? Who doesn't like placing themselves in the middle of a literal shitstorm?"

Garbita opened her mouth, then closed it and settled for a long growl.

Sugressa cleared her throat. "Um. So does anyone have suggestions? Last year when they started up, Glinda tried to intervene and got smacked square in the face. Sent her flipping head over heels."

"It was her own fault," Fecanya said. "What kind of idiot hops in the middle of all that and calls for a ceasefire? She's lucky she has a habit of holding her chins so high, or she'd have probably gotten a mouthful."

"Let's just finish our meal and deal with this quickly," Bloomara said. "If we don't get over there and stop them, it'll catch the attention of the human news media, and there's no telling where *that* would lead."

"Probably on the front of *The Olive*," Fecanya said, referring to the human satire news page.

"We should get going now," Garbita said. "The *sooner* we put a stop to this, the *better*."

"Much as I hate to admit it, Garbage Girl is right. If we don't get there before tomorrow, it'll rain. You do *not* want to deal with this in the rain."

Garbita narrowed her eyes. "For the last time, stop calling me ... what's that?"

Fecanya looked up front her smartphone. "What's what?"

"What are you doing with that contraption, here?"

Fecanya blinked at the other fairy, then looked at the phone in her hand. "This?" She held it up, and the other fairies recoiled as though it was a poisonous snake. "What's the matter with all of you?" "You've clearly taken leave of your wits to bring that thing here," Bloomara gasped.

"The airwaves," Garbita said, near panic. "You'll infect the air with that thing. Get it out of here!"

Fecanya looked at them in open-mouthed fascination. "You're kidding, right?" She looked to her left at Larry. The dwarf shrugged and tore off another hunk of something unrecognizable as food. She looked back to the trio. "It's a phone."

"It's human tech-*no*-logy," Garbita said.

Fecanya laughed, but the others were having none of it. "Un … believable." She tossed the phone into the air and snapped her fingers. The phone disappeared.

* * *

As usual, Bloomara took the lead of their little procession, followed by Garbita, then Sugressa, with Fecanya bringing up the rear. As soon as they'd stepped out of the portal in the middle of the Congo rainforest, they'd noticed everything was eerily quiet.

Garbita stole nervous glances all about them, especially the trees. "I don't like this at *all*."

A quick retort came to mind, but Fecanya kept it to herself. She didn't like the feel of the place either. She wrinkled her lips and pushed them all the way up under her nose. The humid forest was tense and musty. "I'm starting to wonder if we're not traveling through the hairy armpit of one giant gorilla in the first place."

"Better watch your mouth, fairy girl."

The group froze as one, and looked up into the trees in the direction of the voice. Chimpanzees were perched like thugs in the surrounding trees. Several began climbing down toward them.

As six chimps came to the ground and knuckled their way over, Fecanya eyed the lead chimp, taking in his massive arms and coarse black fur. Despite the tense situation, Fecanya bit back her laughter. If ever there was a case that nature had a sense of humor, primates were the proof. At his full height, this chimp stood no taller than three to four feet, yet without a doubt, he could mangle the strongest human in a fight.

"We are hardly *girls*, my good chimp," Bloomara began, and Fecanya closed her eyes. "A little respect would be appreciated."

The lead chimp went into a fit of hopping laughter. The rest of his ground squad followed suit. After the mocking dance routine ended, the lead chimp stood on his considerably short legs, walked up to the fairy supervisor with his arms waving in the air, and stopped in front of her. Bloomara's wand trembled in her sweaty palm, but she held her head high as the chimp looked down on her.

"Here's what this 'good chimp' thinks of your respect." He came back down to his knuckles, and with one leathery hand, grabbed his top lip and flipped it up over his nose.

The other fairies blinked, Bloomara's face flushed, and Fecanya pressed her lips together to keep from laughing.

The lead chimp shook his hairy head at Bloomara, then turned his back to her and hopped up and down. The other chimps imitated their leader, while their comrades in the trees began swinging and screaming laughter, some lying on their thick branch perches with hands on their bellies, mouths agape in hysterics.

The hairy primate galloped a circle around Bloomara before finally calming down.

Fecanya sucked in her teeth at what was sure to be an angry explosion from the supervisor, and stepped forward. "Hey, buddy. Got a name?"

The chimpanzee turned toward her, and she fought the urge to gulp at the sight of those teeth. *I swear if I have to talk to anyone else with large sharp teeth ...*

With a long finger, he flipped his lip down. "Thade."

Fecanya frowned. "Thade?"

He stared at her a moment, then giggled in that high-pitch chimpanzee voice. "Nope. Just playing. It's Kalvin."

Fecanya's mouth fell open, and she covered it up with a nod. *Oh that's much less ridiculous.*

Kalvin knuckled over and offered his hand. Fecanya took it, and warm leathery fingers enveloped hers, and half her forearm as well.

"I'm Fecanya." She pointed to the others. "That's Sugressa, Garbita, and Bloomara."

"What's a bunch of fairies doing skipping around in here?" Kalvin asked.

"We were *not* skipping," Garbita said.

Fecanya gave her a deliberate, wide-eyed look, and the prudish fairy quieted. *I need to fix her up on a date with ole Witless.* "We're just passing through," Fecanya said. "Maybe you can help us. There's news of two arguing gorilla clans ..."

The chimps erupted in hysterics yet again, hopping and screaming in laughter until Kalvin stopped. "It's gotten so big that a bunch of fairies came to watch?"

"We're hoping to stop it from escalating."

Kalvin trembled with laughter. "Think you can wait long enough for me to round up a few more of the fellas? They won't want to miss this."

Fecanya blinked. "Why so?"

"Who wouldn't want to see four fairies covered in—"

"We're hoping to avoid that."

"By getting in the middle of a fight between the Hurlers and—"

Sugressa coughed. "Did you say ... the Hurlers?"

Kalvin laughed. "Yup."

Fecanya almost fainted away. She looked at Bloomara. "We need to get out of here. I don't care how big this blows up."

Bloomara drew herself up to her full just-over-one-foot height. "We will do no such thing. We must put a stop to this nonsense."

The chimps went into another round of violent laughter and antics. Sugressa trembled, Garbita looked at the primates in open disgust, and Fecanya patted the air with her hand.

"You don't get it, Bloom. There's only one group that the Hurlers always get into it with."

"What does that matter?"

Fecanya took a deep breath. "Have you ever heard of the Silverback Spartans?"

Chapter Eight

No." Fecanya shook her head every step on the way to the gorilla territory. "No, no, no. Nope. Nope, nope, nope."

"Will you cut it out," Bloomara snapped. "We've a job to do."

Fecanya just shook her head more vigorously. "Nope."

"You will perform this task as assigned," Bloomara stated. "You are an Ordure Engineer of Fey World Maintenance Services, and it is your job, your *duty*, to assist in the cessation of gorilla hostilities."

"You ever been out here before, Bloom?" Fecanya asked.

"That doesn't change our job …"

"You ever *seen* a fight between two gorilla factions?"

Beside her, Garbita scanned the jungle as though afraid they would be attacked at any moment.

Bloomara sniffed. "What I have or have not seen is irrelevant …"

"You ever seen a Hurler gorilla throw?" Fecanya interrupted. "If humans ever got wind of it, they'd start recruiting them for baseball."

"What does that have to do with anything?"

Fecanya threw her hands in the air. "How can you be this dense?" She waggled a finger at the Garbage Fairy. "Okay, fine. You get smacked in the back of the head by a high velocity turd and get back to me."

"We can't just let this happen, Fecanya." It was Sugressa that spoke. "We have to show them that violence isn't the answer."

Fecanya laughed. "Sure thing, Miss Sugar Spice Girl. You ever seen a fight involving a clan of Spartan gorillas?"

"What's a Spartan gorilla?"

Fecanya's laughter turned incredulous. "We're done." He shoulders drooped. "I never thought it would end like this ... death by speeding stool."

"Will you stop it, already?" Garbita said. "You're making us all nervous."

"I can't believe Hard-Ass sent me here with you three."

"Don't say that, Fecanya," Sugressa said. "It won't be that bad. We stick together and work together, and it'll be fine."

Fecanya gave her a blank look.

"Mouths shut," Bloomara said, and Fecanya glared at the back of her head, imagining what it would look like caked in a Hurler turd. "Shush, I say. I hear something."

"Probably your own loud breathing," Fecanya muttered.

As they approached an incline, Fecanya heard it, too. Yelling, roaring, orders being shouted, and the rapid thuds that could be nothing other than chest-beating.

Fecanya heard the distinct sound of giggling again. It wasn't the local chimps—who were no doubt snickering in the surrounding trees—but the same giggling she'd heard in the alley, back in Garmon. She looked at the other three, but they gave no sign of having heard anything.

The Fey World Maintenance fairies looked at one another, then up the hill. Bloomara signaled for them to creep up.

"Can't we just write them a letter or something?" Fecanya whispered. "Violence is never the answer, or something like that?"

"I've asked you several times to be quiet," Bloomara replied, "and you haven't changed that behavior. I imagine a clan of angry gorillas are almost as difficult.

Garbita tittered into her hand, and Fecanya "tripped" on a hidden root and smacked the garbage fairy in the hand. The move caused Garbita to punch herself in the mouth with a high-pitched grunt. Her head snapped back, causing her green bun to dislodge into a sloppy pile on top of her head.

"That's it!" Garbita balled up her fist and took a swing at Fecanya, who ducked the left hook and stepped back.

"Hey, sorry! I didn't see that pesky root!"

Fecanya bit her top lip as Garbita glared at her, but the bubbling laugher seeped through in the form of long snort.

Garbita bared her teeth. "Ooooh, OOOH!" She took another swing at Fecanya, who easily leaned away, and the garbage fairy followed up with a right hook.

"Stop it," Bloomara whispered through clenched teeth. "You'll alert the whole damned rainforest!"

Garbita heard none of it. The remains of her neatly tucked bun bounced at an angle off the side of her head, strands waving in the air as she swung her fists at Fecanya, who ducked and skittered away.

Sugressa came in from the side, and wrapped her arms around Garbita, but the green-haired fairy continued to swing at Fecanya.

"Geez! Relax, garbage girl," Fecanya said, holding up her hands in placating gesture. "Don't get your wings in a crinkle."

Bloomara stepped between them. "Will ... you ... shut ... UP. You'll bring the whole damned clan of smelly ..."

Fecanya didn't have to guess why Bloom had stopped talking. She watched five hulking reasons materialize out of the brush all around them. "Fantastic."

*   *   *

41

"... *Sloths*," Fecanya improvised. "I know, Bloom! I'm sorry. I know the smelly sloths will come down here if we don't shut up. Sorry!"

"That's insulting to sloths," Sugressa whispered from the corner of her mouth.

"Right. What're the sloths gonna do to us?" Fecanya whispered back. "Slow us to death?"

A giant silverback gorilla knuckled his way forward. The four fairies bounced with each step of the hulking primate.

"Will you let *go* of me," Garbita growled, and finally extricated herself from Sugressa.

"Mmm. Clan of smelly sloths, eh?" the gorilla said. He stopped in front of Bloomara, who had to bend backwards to look up at the giant silverback.

"I ... er, yes, of course," Bloomara said. "Those darned smelly sloths." She waved her hands in the air. "For all we know, they could be converging on us now; right this very second."

The gorilla's nostrils flared and he lowered himself to have a closer look at the Bloom Fairy. "Sloths don't travel in clans."

"Er, are you sure?" Bloomara asked. "One can never be sure with the unpredictable creatures."

The gorilla inhaled, then puffed out through his nostrils. Bloomara's blue bun unraveled in the gust, and fell disheveled about her shoulders. "A fairy," the gorilla boomed, though he spoke in a calm voice.

Beside her, Fecanya felt her chest cavity vibrate.

"Why are you here?"

"I ... we ..." Bloomara's mouth bobbed open and closed several times.

"You are here to pretend to be a fish?" the gorilla asked.

"We're here to visit," Fecanya said, shoving her supervisor out of the way. She forced her terror down at standing in front of the massive primate. "We wish to speak with the mighty Spartan Clan."

"We're busy," the gorilla said. "No time for fairy visits."

Fecanya took a deep breath. "I'm Fecanya, Ordure Engineer of Fey World Maintenance Services. We were sent to speak with you, if you please."

The gorilla stared at her for a long time, then blinked. "A dookie fairy?" He leaned sideways to look around her, though Fecanya knew perfectly well he could see every inch around her. "I don't see no shovel. How do you clean up?"

Fecanya's jaw moved side to side as she ground her teeth. "I have other methods. Please, we need to speak to your clan chief. It's very important."

"Told you. We got no time for fairy visits."

"We understand, er, I didn't get your name."

"I didn't give it." The gorilla offered a long-fingered hand. "Bruce."

Fecanya looked at that massive hand and wondered where it had recently been. She swallowed the bile in her throat and placed her hand in it. The giant, soft, leathery hand closed around her arm, and part of her shoulder, and lifted her up and down from the ground.

When he let her go, Fecanya looked at her arm as though it was a foreign object. It felt several degrees warmer than the rest of her body.

"What do you want?" Bruce asked.

"A shower," Fecanya muttered.

"Huh?"

"To speak with the leader of your clan, please. It's most important."

Bruce grumbled as he considered this. The surrounding gorillas were firm in their positions, unmoving sentries ready to explode into action at any moment. They were the living embodiment of humanity's precarious position, should the great apes decide to get organized.

"Very well. Come."

They followed Bruce up the hill, his small force falling in around their fairy visitors. They crested the hill and started down. Once Bruce was far enough down for them to see over his head, Garbita and Sugressa gasped. Bloomara said, "Oh, my."

Fecanya groaned.

At the base of the hill in an open area was a cluster of gorillas, their silver backs shining up at the watching fairies. They were in a phalanx formation, and with each move, the gorilla warriors gave a powerful shout. To the right, another group formed a circular formation, with warriors positioned in the middle. When all were in place, the gorillas that made up the rim of the circle crouched and pressed their forearms together in a defensive position. The gorillas standing a little higher, did the same, but at an angle over the head of their crouching companions. The gorillas in the middle stood up to their full height, and did the same on top.

"Turtle formation," one of their escorts rumbled at Fecanya, and signaled for them to keep moving.

"It really does look like a turtle," Sugressa said. "That's amazing!"

Their gorilla escort swelled with pride, and knuckled their way down the hill with heads a little higher.

"I can't even see anyone inside that big dome of *hair*-y forearms," Garbita said.

"That's the point," Bruce called from further down. Won't nothing penetrate that formation."

When they reached the base of the hill, they were met by another soldier whose posture indicated that he outranked Bruce.

"Why do you bring a troupe of fairies into our camp?" the gorilla demanded of Bruce.

"Troupe?" Bloomara replied in indignation.

Fecanya eyed the supervisor. "You do realize all he'd need to do is raise his hand and let it drop on your head, and you'd be as flat as your feet."

"I do *not* have flat feet!"

"Shut up!" Bruce snapped over his shoulder, then turned back to his superior. "They claim it's very important that they see King Leo."

"And you just bring them here, like that?"

Bruce waved a giant hand in their direction. "How often do fairies come?"

The other gorilla thought about that, then nodded and called to a smaller, younger soldier. After grunting orders at the boy, Bruce sent him off.

Fecanya watched the training apes while they waited. One, who was smaller than Bruce, picked up a log big enough around for her to make a home out of, and threw it at least a couple dozen feet. The log hit the ground with an earth-vibrating thud, and the gorilla pounded his chest.

"We shouldn't be here," Garbita said.

"Reeaally?" Fecanya placed her hand over her chest. "You think?"

Impossible as it seemed, an even bigger gorilla approached the group to tower over Bruce, who bent his giant arms as he bowed in obeisance. "King Leo."

The gorilla king nodded, and Bruce straightened. Well, a gorilla's version of straightening, anyway. "I'm told that we have visitors."

Bruce moved aside and indicated the four fairies, three of which took a discrete step back, until Fecanya was at the front of the group.

She glared over her shoulder at the others. When she looked back at the king, she saw amusement in his wise eyes. He had two long scars down the left side of his face that continued halfway down his chest. His furry forearms looked like someone had attached barrels to them, so big and round they were. But these barrels had thick cords of muscle.

"I take it that you've been designated as the spokesfairy for this little band?"

"Apparently so," Fecanya grumbled. "We represent Fey World Maintenance Services ..."

King Leo nodded. "I've heard of it. Had occasional visits over the years. State your business, spokesfairy of Fey World Maintenance Services."

Fecanya saw in the old King's eyes that he likely knew what they'd come for, but allowed them to present their case anyway. "FWMS is concerned that the ensuing and escalating hostility between the Silverback Spartans and the Hurlers may attract human attention. We've been sent to implore you to find a more civil method to put this to rest, and to assist in facilitating this alternative."

King Leo grinned. "Your concern is appreciated, but the Hurlers have steadily encroached on our territory. Three of my scouts met with a rather aggressive bombardment when they confronted a band of them."

"We intend to speak with them after we leave here."

"That shouldn't be difficult," King Leo replied. "They're on their way."

Fecanya ran through her memory of everything she'd concerning the two clans. Despite what humans believed about their numbers, gorillas were particularly good at hiding them. The Hurlers were over five hundred strong. She doubted these Spartan gorillas had that number. But then, given their name, and reports of their sneaking into human villages at night to watch television through the windows, she could probably guess the exact number of warriors in King Leo's force.

"Erm. How ... how many soldiers do you plan to take? The Hurlers have a huge army."

The angry scar on King Leo's face bent as he smiled. We will meet them with three hundred of our best soldiers."

Fecanya tried not to roll her eyes, and smiled. *Of course.* She figured she might as well go through with this little dialogue so the king could get it out of his system. "But you're *horribly* out-*numbered*, great King Leo," she said in her most dramatic voice.

The king straightened up to his full height and thrust his fist in the air. "GORILAAAAAS! WHAT IS YOUR PROFESSIOOOON?"

46

Every silver-backed Spartan gorilla stopped what they were doing, turned to face King Leo, and pounded their chests. "HA-OOH!"

Fecanya heard Sugressa squeak behind her, and she couldn't blame the Sugar Fairy. There wasn't a human alive that could produce a roar like a gorilla, nor was there one with the teeth to brandish as well. It was quite terrifying.

"You see, little sprite. We are fewer, yet still we outnumber them." He turned to Bruce. "We move."

As the gorillas organized into formation, Fecanya tried again. "The damage to the local vegetation will be traumatizing."

"They will survive," the king replied. "Does that not fall within your job description, Ordure Engineer?"

The thought of dealing with a fecal fallout of such magnitude was enough to make Fecanya's wings shrivel. "Please, King Leo. We can find a better way to resolve this problem without any injury to gorilla or plant. Please, think of the poor innocent plants."

The Silverback Spartan King moved closer and smiled down at her. "All will be for the best, little sprite. The Hurlers will retreat back to their own lands, or we will pound them into it." He started away. "You are welcome to join us or run along home."

Fecanya looked to Bloomara.

The Bloom Fairy's shoulders sagged. "If we cannot avert this, there will be much to clean, and many injured plants to rehabilitate."

They fell in with the gorillas, who'd taken a rectangular formation.

Fecanya wondered if she could find a job at another facility, but that thought ended with a resigned sigh. It was no use. All the Fey World Maintenance Service Centers shared information in their global network. If she abandoned her job, word would reach any prospective facility in short order. She glared at the stupid gorillas heading toward their stupid impending battle.

"This is really gonna suck."

Chapter Nine

Seeing two giant clans of silver-backed gorillas facing off in an open space just outside a forest canopy was a sight to behold. Especially when you're only a foot tall. To the four fairies, it was like watching two giant herds of dinosaurs squaring off.

"We're going to get trampled," Garbita moaned.

"Only if you're stupid enough to run out in the middle of them," Fecanya replied. She regarded King Leo. "May we address the King of the Hurlers before you all begin your ... thing?"

"Of course, little sprite."

Fecanya started forward, then noticed she was alone. She glanced over her shoulder at the others, who hadn't budged. "You gonna come out here and help?"

Bloomara sniffed. "You obviously have this under control. Have at it."

"Deliah sent four of us."

"And we're all here."

"Um, that's not fair, Bloomara."

The supervisor smiled at her. "Life isn't fair."

Fecanya couldn't disagree. Her job was proof of that. She gave Bloomara a toothy grin and snapped her fingers. Her iBerry phone winked into existence and dropped in her hand. "I love these things. They've got video recording capabilities."

Bloomara glared daggers at Fecanya, and shuffled up beside her. "Lead on, Ordure Engineer."

With more than a little hesitation, they moved into the middle of the field between the two large forces of gorillas. Fecanya strained to pick out the king in the mass of lumbering muscle that was the Hurlers.

Laughter began to ripple about the Hurler ranks until one voice boomed above it all. "What's this? The Spartan Clan uses fairies to do their fighting, now? Have you sunk so low, old king?"

Fecanya swallowed and slowly turned to see the Silverback Spartan Clan, standing shoulder to shoulder, foot-hand to knuckle, without so much as a blink. She suspected an army of terra-cotta warriors would have moved more.

She turned back to the Hurler Clan, wondering if they understood the pounding they were welcoming. "We'd like to speak with your king, if you please."

"Who do you think's talking, sprite?" the booming voice said.

The Hurler ranks parted to admit a male that was even bigger than King Leo. The ground thudded as the hulking brute moved toward them. Fecanya wanted nothing more than to move away, even though he was still across the field.

"I am SFC! What do you want, little sprite?"

"SFC?" Garbita whispered.

"Super Fighting Championship," Fecanya replied from the corner of her mouth. "Gorillas sneak into human villages and watch television through the windows."

"Ah." Garbita frowned. "Well … that explains the Spartan gorillas, but doesn't this fellow know that SFC is an organization and not an actual individual?"

"You want to go tell him?" Fecanya asked. She cleared her throat again. "Mighty King SFC. We've been sent by Fey World Maintenance Services …"

51

"Fey World Meddling Services, more like it," the gorilla interrupted. Chuckling sounded from both sides.

No matter what happens, I'm redirecting some of your ammo into your face, you swayback bastard. She forced a titter. "Very clever, mighty King SFC. We've been sent in hopes of assisting in a peaceful conclusion to this conflict between your two clans."

SFC motioned toward King Leo. "Just tell the old man over there to pack up his buddies and get out of here. There's your peaceful conclusion."

King Leo's ranks didn't need to part for him to approach, for he was already at the front of his ranks. "How far did you come to try and take our home? When you first arrived here, you were welcomed. We thought you'd come to share this rainforest. But you only take more and more. You will not run us out. You can live here in peace, or you can go back to where you came from."

"Not for you to dictate," SFC replied. "We Hurlers live where we want. And we want to live here. You can make way or we will move you."

King Leo's nostrils flared.

The bigger gorilla moved forward until he was towering over the Silverback Spartan. "You look like you want to challenge me in a cage match, little king."

Fecanya's mouth crinkled. *You keep up this nonsense, and the humans will give you all the cage you can handle, potbelly.* "Come on, boys. Surely there's a way to resolve this. You're both grown gorillas, here." She looked at SFC. "Are there so many of you that you need to take more land?"

SFC looked down his leathery nose at her. "This land is what we want."

In spite of the close proximity of the other gorilla, King Leo smiled. "Not all unions are destined, young King. Marie did not want to marry you. How many times must this come up?"

Fecanya would have vomited if she wasn't standing in the middle of two armies of aggressively perspiring primates bent on pounding each other. All this because SFC was rejected by the king's daughter? Was this a joke?

"You are king!" SFC replied. "Your word is supposed to be law. What kind of king are you if your own daughter will not obey your will?"

"It is because I am a good king that my people can make choices for themselves," Leo replied. "Marie did not wish to marry you."

"You are weak," SFC declared, and his forces rumbled in agreement. "Old and weak. It's time for a new king. Where once our clans could have been joined through my marriage to your daughter, I will now cast you aside and your clan will be absorbed into mine."

"If you manage that," King Leo said, "you'll find yourself in the worst fight of your life, young king. We gorillas are a peaceful folk. Perhaps the little sprite is right. We should settle this peacefully."

Fecanya's mouth dropped open, and she snapped it shut before either of the gorillas saw. True, the giant primates were normally peaceful. But these? One clan was obsessed with Super Fighting Championship, and the other, a movie about 300 Spartans. Peaceful? They were insane. All of them.

"Think carefully, young king," Leo said. The power behind the warning in his voice made Fecanya shudder. She looked over her shoulder at the others, who looked as though they were ready to bolt.

SFC scowled down at the older, smaller gorilla. "You are the one who should think carefully, old king. Our dung will fly high, and blot out the sun!"

Behind King SFC, the Hurler force roared in challenge, thrusting giant fists into the air.

Fecanya sighed.

At the front of his quiet, disciplined force, King Leo smiled.

"Then we will pound you in the shade."

Chapter Ten

King SFC's eyes widened. "You've gone crazy, old king. Look at your force, and look at mine! We outnumber you twice over. This is madness!"

King Leo half turned to look at his force of three hundred gorillas, then back at the bigger king. "You come here, threatening us with servitude ..."

"They're threatening you with shit ..." Fecanya said dryly.

"... and the usurpation of my rule." A smile crept across King Leo's face. "Madness? No, SFC. This isn't madness. This ... IS ... SPAR—"

"Alright alright, al*right*."

Fecanya gave a little hop, and her wings fluttered as she hovered between the two kings. "You!" She pointed in the Hurler King's face. "Will you *please* stop feeding him lines? If this is gonna be a happy fun-time film quote contest, ditch the army, steal a TV, and play nice!"

She turned to King Leo. "And you! I ... just ..." she shook her head and turned back to SFC, just in time to see a giant black hand slowly push her aside. "Hey!"

"Your little sprite has more spunk than you, old king."

Leo stared into the younger gorilla's eyes, and though she was now hovering at the side of the confrontation, Fecanya saw a flicker of trepidation from the Hurler King. She didn't blame him. "Old" King Leo was a legend in gorilla society. Even if it wasn't a general rule that the smaller members of the fey world were adept at global meddling, it would have been hard not to have heard the name of King Leo. Just the sight of him was proof enough that he'd seen his share of fighting.

Fecanya looked down at her companions, all frozen with fear. *I'm so glad Hard-Ass sent me a trio of champions to have my back.* "Guys, please. This doesn't have to happen. Gorillas aren't supposed to fight like this. Yeah, the occasional teeth-bearing, or turd slinging can happen between any species. But you're better than this. You're acting like ... like *humans.*"

That gave both primates pause, and a cloud of shame passed over King Leo's face. "Perhaps you have a point, little sprite." He looked up at SFC. "Might we come to an agreement, Hurler King? Let us behave like civilized gorillas."

SFC puffed out his chest, and in that moment, Fecanya knew she was going to be cleaning up endless acres of scattered shit.

"No, old king. You've openly displayed your weakness. Prepare yourself."

The Hurler king turned away, leaving the fairies and King Leo alone in the middle of the field.

Fecanya turned an apologetic look on the Spartan king. "Sorry. I guess I'm not the best negotiator."

The silverback king smiled. "Your concern is noted, but worry not, little sprite. No Silverback Spartan dies today."

Fecanya's left eye twitched. *When have gorillas ever fought to the death en masse?* "Oh that's good to know."

"Well that was a lackluster effort," Bloomara stated when Leo turned away.

55

"Oh?" Fecanya placed the tips of her fingers over her chest in mock concern. "I'm sorry if I gave the impression help wasn't welcome. You could've opened up that cookie coffin beneath your nose at any time and spoken up."

Sugressa giggled.

Garbita hid her grin behind her fingers and looked away.

Bloomara's face flushed, but before she could offer a haughty retort, Sugressa pointed toward the Hurlers. "Uh oh. They're starting up."

"Perhaps we shouldn't be standing here," Garbita said.

"You mean you don't want to get smacked with shit from both sides?" Fecanya replied. "Then yeah, we'd better go."

"Why *are* you so ill-mannered?"

"Why *ahh* you so ill-*mah*-nered? Just get to the sidelines, Garbage Girl." Fecanya took off toward the Spartan gorillas before the fuming fairy could respond.

Like any brave leader, King Leo stood at the front of his force, giving last minute orders. He half turned at her approach. "There is nothing left to discuss, little sprite. We fight, this day." He turned to his force of three hundred gorillas. "THIS, IS WHERE WE FIGHT!" He pointed across the field. "THAT, IS WHERE THEY CRY!"

The gorilla force gave a big cry of, "HA-OOH!"

Fecanya looked at all of them. *They're insane. Every, single, one of them.* She turned and flew to the bushes where the other fairies stood.

"No luck?" Sugressa asked.

"Shit's gonna fly," Fecanya replied, looking out at the field.

King SFC barked an order, and the Hurlers beat their chests and pounded the ground. They roared and snarled, and Fecanya felt a fresh flush of terror.

"I'm a Sugar Fairy!" Sugressa squeaked. "Why am I here? I'm not trained for this. It isn't my job!"

Fecanya resisted the urge to mock the girl. She really did like Sugressa, but then, who couldn't like her. She was a sugar fairy. Fecanya's eyes widened. Sugar Fairy!

The two clans charged across the field.

"Hey, Cloy."

"Fecanya," Sugressa said in a plaintive voice. "Would you please not call me that? I don't like it."

Fecanya sighed. "Sorry. Look, you're a Sugar Fairy. You know, spreading sweetness and all that? Maybe you're here to sweeten these goons up so they don't want to fight. Maybe you should be doing the negotiating and not me."

"There's an idea," Garbita muttered. "A Sugar Fairy might just be a better influence to hostilities than a Shit Fairy."

"Thahn ah Sheeeet Faireh," Fecanya mocked, while Sugressa giggled into her hands. "And why do you think you're here, Garbage Girl? Who do you think will be helping me clean up, if this fight gets ugly?"

"I'm afraid she's right," Bloomara said.

Garbita turned to the supervisor and offered a toothy smile.

Fecanya thought Garbita might actually bite Bloomara with all those teeth. She pointed toward the field. "Here we go."

The Hurlers charged, howling and pounding the ground, while the Spartans simply led a controlled charge while chanting, "HA-OOH, HA-OOH, HA-OOH!"

The two clans clashed, but instead of a tangled mass of fists and biting teeth, the Hurlers did a sort of skipping stop just before collision.

Fecanya snorted. It reminded her of the time she witnessed a supposed schoolyard fight, when two boys sprinted toward each other, then had second thoughts the instant before impact.

The Spartan gorillas stopped and waited as the Hurlers snarled and pounded the ground, feinting lunges and beating their chests.

Fecanya watched in disbelief. The whole display would have been terrifying if they hadn't practically tilled the ground to avoid actually throwing a punch.

The Spartans had seen it as well, for they stood their ground, watching the display with admirable discipline. How they didn't fall into fits of howling laughter, Fecanya couldn't imagine. She did, however, hear screaming laughter from further in the jungle that could only have come from Kalvin and his watching chimpanzees.

Finally, King SFC emerged from the middle of the "fight" and challenged King Leo.

"This should be interesting," Garbita said, and for once, Fecanya agreed.

Without preamble, the Hurler king launched himself into a wild show of aggression, baring his teeth, darting to and fro, rolling his shoulders, and pounding the ground and his chest. Throughout the display, King Leo stood there on feet and knuckles, watching in thinly veiled boredom.

The show went on for a few more moments until mighty King SFC made a mistake. In his wild flurry, he misjudged the distance between them, and accidentally struck King Leo in the chin.

"Uh, oooooh," Sugressa said, and Fecanya, Garbita, and Bloomara nodded in unison.

King Leo's head snapped backward and the entire non-battling army froze.

The old king rubbed his chin with a surprised look, while King SFC made an expression as one would right before the doctor gave them a needle.

King Leo's shoulders bounced as he chuckled, and just as SFC joined in the humor, the old king's giant arm flashed out.

Everyone reared back in surprise, for it happened so fast, nobody registered the movement.

Meaty fist connected with not-firm-enough belly, and King SFC doubled over with a mighty exhale, like the sound like a lion exhaling a hairball.

The king of the Hurlers folded in half, holding his hands to his stomach as he sank into the ground like melted butter, and curled into a little ball.

A wave of uncertainty washed over the Hurler army as gorilla heads swiveled this way and that. Finally, two Hurler soldiers lumbered forward. They looked in askance at King Leo, who nodded. The two Hurlers bent their massive arms in an awkward bow, then lifted the compressed ball that was SFC, and carried him away.

Out of Ordure

Chapter Eleven

Fecanya gave a great exhale of relief that caught in her throat at the sound of SFC's strangled voice. In one last act of idiocy, the Hurler king, still curled in a ball over his soldiers' heads, threw up his hand. "Cheap shot. Don't let him get away with that. Your king was dealt a cheap shot."

At those words, the collective brain of the Hurler army went on autopilot. They whooped and hollered, beating their chests as they closed ranks around the retreating king.

"That's it! I've had it!" It was Bruce who'd spoken. The poor Hurler who was his adversary didn't have a chance. Bruce's fist snapped out in an uppercut so impressive, Fecanya half expected the Spartan gorilla to launch spinning into the air.

The Hurler's feet left the ground, and he crashed on top of several of his companions. Whatever fight was left in the Hurlers, fled with their comrade's consciousness. At that, the Hurlers broke ranks and took off, and the Spartans, as one, stood to their full height and pounded one fist to their chests. "HA-OOH! HA-OOH! HA-OOH!"

Once again, Fecanya was about to exhale in relief, when she noted the odd running posture of the fleeing Hurlers.

"What are they doing?" Garbita asked. "Why are they running like that?"

"It looks weird," Sugressa remarked.

Fecanya felt a cold chill go down her spine. "Oh no. No. No no no."

There was only one reason a clan of Hurlers would run on two feet, half-turned, with one hand curled behind them.

"Oh my goodness," Bloomara said. "They wouldn't. They're not...."

"Stay here and find out," Fecanya said, and she bolted for the trees. The others were right behind her, and they had just reached a thick clump of shrubbery when the forest echoed with the sound of rapid flatulence.

"Did they just ..."

"Yes!" Fecanya said as she dove for the shrubbery.

She felt a shoulder crash into her back, followed by a grunt. A foot smacked her on the nose, and she was sure a knee found its way under her armpit. "Urgh. Get *off*!"

The fairies struggled in a tangle of arms and legs in the bushes, then froze at the sound of King Leo's voice.

"Gori*llaaas*! Formay-sh*uuuun*!"

Fecanya squirmed her way out of the tangle and peeked through the bushes. The Spartan gorillas had formed an impressive dome of solid forearms. She couldn't help but admire the perfect formation, until she looked to the right of the field. To the right, and up.

"Un ... believable."

It seemed the Hurler king hadn't been bluffing when he said their biological projectiles would block the sun, for a shadow did indeed cover the field.

Fecanya poked her hands out of the shrubs and went to work.

"What are you doing?" Sugressa asked.

Fecanya barely heard the question. She focused on the incoming wave of gorilla turds, and managed to cause the first few rows to decompose and fall to spread harmlessly on the ground and absorb into the soil. Sweat trickled down the side of her face as she worked.

"You can do it, Fecanya!" Sugressa said from behind.

Row after row of flying feces decayed into powder and absorbed into the soil, and she could have sworn she'd heard the sound of many irritated voices, growling in unison. It sounded just like the inhuman giggling voices she'd heard earlier.

She blocked out the strange sound and focused fully on her work. But it was too much. An entire army of gorillas had unleashed this assault, and it was beyond any single fairy to handle. Fecanya fell back into the bush and scooted as far to the other side as she could, then curled into a tiny ball, much like King SFC had done.

*   *   *

Fecanya squeezed her eyes shut, and clamped her hands over her mouth and nose to block out the horrible sounds—and smells—of waste warfare going on just outside their shrubbery bunker. It seemed to go on forever until finally, mercifully, the last splat sounded, and all went quiet.

For a time, she remained where she was, curled in a little ball, until enough time passed and all was silent. She finally opened her eyes and blinked, then uncurled and tentatively climbed to her feet.

"Is it over?" Garbita asked. She, too, had curled up, along with the others. Beyond all reasonable hope, bushes had provided adequate cover. Fecanya crept out like a skittish deer, eyes scanning left to right. She swayed on her feet when the sight—and smell—hit her.

All about the battlefield were leaves and twigs. Even some of the smaller saplings had been felled under the assault. And the ground ... the ground was so covered, she couldn't even see it.

Bloomara climbed out next. "I suppose now that it's over we can ... oh, by mother Lilith herself!"

Garbita climbed out next, and gasped. Which was a mistake.

Sugressa climbed out beside the vomiting Detritus Redistributor, and fainted away.

Fecanya sighed. "Guess I'd better get started."

She'd barely taken two steps when she heard grumbling to the side, and looked over at the forgotten Spartan gorillas. They were just breaking their turtle shell formation. Those who were unlucky enough to have formed the outer dome were shaking their forearms, casting angry looks in the direction the Hurlers had fled.

Fecanya started to her task, then hesitated when she spotted a very angry Leo. The king looked as though he could have ground rocks to dust in those gnashing teeth. "Gori*llaaas*! Prepare for glory!"

"Somebody wake her up," Fecanya said, waving a hand at Sugressa. She turned to the task of breaking down the dung in a path toward the giant primates, who were rapidly transitioning from anger to rage. "Get her over here!" Fecanya hissed.

"I'm coming," Sugressa said. She sounded tired. Fecanya felt sorry for the Sugar Fairy. She'd never witnessed such horror, and in fact, this was the exact opposite of her job description.

"Alright, girl. Best put on your big fairy pants and get to talking." Fecanya cleared the last few feet between them and King Leo, and shoved Sugressa forward.

The angry king held up a hand to forestall them. "Save your efforts, little sprite. They will pay for this day."

As Sugressa worked to talk Leo down, Fecanya went about her task. She listened with half an ear as Sugressa, true to her profession, sweet-talked the gorillas back to calm. She made them laugh, and promised to work out a deal with a local bee community to provide a little bit of sweetener to their meals for the next month.

"Little sprite," Fecanya heard from over her shoulder. She turned to see King Leo waving her over. "You truly intend to clean all this?" He waved a hand—that surely weighed more than all four fairies combined—at the disgusting battlefield.

Fecanya rolled her tongue around the inside of her cheek. "Yeah. That's what I'm here for."

Leo smiled. "I offer you my thanks, and the thanks of all Silverback Spartans." He lifted his head and shouted, "Gori*llaaas!*"

The force of three hundred gorillas turned to face the tiny fairies, and gave a single thump of their right fists to their chests. "HA-OOH! Thank youuu."

Fecanya smiled. She'd never felt so appreciated before. "You're welcome, King Leo." She waved to all of the smiling gorillas. "You're all welcome!"

Bloomara walked between Fecanya and Sugressa, and placed a hand on each of their shoulders. "Well done! There shall be a gleaming report on Deliah's desk for each of you!"

Try as she might, Fecanya couldn't stop her widening grin. "Um. Thanks, Bloom."

Bloomara nodded. "Well earned."

"I guess I should get to work, so we can be done." Fecanya looked down to hide her embarrassment at all the attention, and noticed something. "What's that?"

Bloomara's smile faded. "What's what?"

"That." Fecanya pointed a trembling finger at the end of her dress. At a tiny brown spot. "Is that … is that … shit?"

Garbita waved her hands gently in the air in front of Fecanya. "Now, now. There's nothing to be concerned about. It's just a little spot—"

"This is shit." Fecanya held the bottom of her dress out to arms-length, staring at the little brown spot as though it were the entrails of a fallen Hurler. It may as well have been. "This is shit. This is *shit*. Get it off me!"

Out of Ordure

Chapter Twelve

Look, I don't know. I just … lost it." Fecanya lay on the on the couch, staring blankly at the ceiling. "I saw all that shit on my dress and just … lost it." She lifted her chin defiantly. "But I still got my job done after they woke me up. By the time we left, that entire field was fertilized to perfection. I'm sure a nice new patch of healthy trees will burst from the ground, reaching for the heavens in short order."

Leowitriss adjusted his spectacles on the tip of his nose and consulted his notes. "It says here that you and Sugressa did a commendable job at minimizing the hostilities, and preventing a prolonged conflict. It also says that you took a lead role in the attempt to reach an agreement between the two clans. That's fantastic, Miss Fecanya. You should be proud of yourself."

She stared at him for a moment, then blinked. "You're not going to kiss me or anything, are you?"

"I … What?" Leowitriss frowned down at her. "What are you …" he regained his composure. "I understand showing happiness may be uncomfortable for you, Miss Fecanya, but this is a safe space."

Fecanya ran her hand over the couch, then looked down at the material. "Is this crushed velvet?"

Leowitriss cleared his throat. "Let's not get off track. We're making progress." He consulted his folder again. "We really must address your fecal phobia."

Fecanya frowned. "It's not a phobia, Leo. I got a bunch of crap on my dress."

"By all accounts, it was a small bit, Fecanya."

"Seemed more like the whole bottom of my dress, if you ask me."

"Do you think that perhaps, your mind embellished the situation due to the possibility you have a fecal phobia?"

"Maybe you didn't hear me the first time. It's not a phobia. I just prefer not to have shit all over me. I can't speak for anyone else, but that's me. Don't like it. Don't want to wear it."

"I understand you wouldn't want it on you, but is it not reasonable to expect this might happen, given your profession?"

"Garbita magically processes garbage," Fecanya said. "I don't see her swimming in it."

"But she doesn't have a panic attack if some of it gets on her, either."

"Yeah sure. We can trade jobs and I'll gladly swim in all the garbage you can fit into one place."

The satyr therapist studied her. "How long have you felt this strongly about your job?"

Fecanya slowly turned her head and stared at the therapist.

"I ... process ... shit."

*   *   *

Fecanya walked out of the office and started toward the Rotunda. After a long day in a musty rainforest, talking with a bunch of hostile, funky gorillas, then cleaning up an entire field of gorilla crap, all she wanted to do was sleep for a few years. Perhaps she could leverage Bloomara's glowing report into some time off.

She scowled. Just the thought of asking Lieutenant Commander Hard-Ass for anything was enough to make her nauseous.

"Why the long face, Fecanya?" Sugressa trotted up from behind as Fecanya turned down a hallway glittering with pixie dust.

"Just got out of another session with ole Leowitless. I'm ready for a nap until, oh, maybe next year. Or year after."

"Aw sweetie. I can't imagine what you're feeling. You obviously have the hardest job here, and likely the least appreciated."

If those words had come from anyone else, Fecanya would have thought them suspiciously patronizing. But Sugressa didn't know how to be anything other than the nicest fairy she'd ever met. It was endearing and sickening at the same time. "Thanks for that."

They passed a clump of miner goblins arguing with a group of dwarves over proper tunneling equipment and hygiene.

"I'll never understand why they work together," Sugressa said, looking back at them. "They always argue."

Fecanya shrugged. "Goblins are born stinking. Dwarves are born arguing, and when they work, they start stinking and never stop. They're perfect for each other." They reached the Rotunda and stopped at the edge of the walkway. "Well I guess ..." she turned to Sugressa and noticed the other fairy's hesitant look. "What?"

"I'm afraid I have some news, Fecanya."

"I'm afraid of having to hear it," Fecanya replied. "What now? Every gorilla in the world took a dump all at once and threw it in one direction? Previously undiscovered giant bear species with inherent diarrhea? Genetically modified dinosaur accidentally eats all the merchandise in a laxative distribution center?"

"Um. Well, no." Sugressa fidgeted and slid a lock of pink hair behind her ear. "Remember that new mega wastewater treatment plant being built in Garmon City?"

Fecanya felt a tremor go down her spine. "Please tell me it's not shutting down or anything."

"Um, no. But there may be a slight problem."

"Slight."

"It may not be as stable as the engineers think."

"It's made by humans, Sugressa. How stable could it be?"

"Deliah wants us to go have a look."

Fecanya visibly deflated. She snapped her fingers, and a lit sweet bark cigarette appeared in front of her. "And all I wanted was to go to my room and pretend not to exist for a few years." She took a long inhale, held it, then blew out a purple cloud. "When am I supposed to go?"

"First thing in the morning."

"Of course."

"I ..." Sugressa continued to fidget. "I told her I'd accompany you, if you wished it. That's why she sent me to deliver the message instead of by slot mail."

It wasn't often that Fecanya was at a loss for words, but that did the job. She took one last draw, then flicked the butt into the air. With snap of her fingers, it burst into tiny purple sparks. "You ... want to come with me?" she asked, her words coming out in purple puffs. "You want to come to a potentially unstable wastewater treatment plant? Have you ever been to one of those things? I'd say they're pretty much anathema to anything related to you."

"You can't go by yourself," Sugressa replied. "And you and Garbita don't much get along. So I figured I'd be the best person to help." She made a bouncy show of shrugging her shoulders. It made the pink bun on top of her head bounce. "Besides. It'll be fun! We get to spy on humans."

"Spying on humans is depressing," Fecanya said. "*Humans* are depressing. Their societal structures, hierarchies, concept of money." She was on a roll. "Their problems, and most of the solutions to their problems just lead to other problems ..."

"Well," Sugressa interjected. "They're sometimes clumsy. It's fun watching how graceful they're not."

Fecanya conceded that with a nod. "I guess so. But trust me. If you spend too much time around them, you start having a horrible outlook on life. It can affect your magic, too. Ever want to weaken someone's magic. Make them spend a lot of time with humans. Wink it right out. Trust me."

Sugressa twitched her lips. It was cute and annoying at the same time. "Oh, they're not that bad. I've seen some really nice humans. And their children are nice."

"Their children are demented sadists that derive pleasure from tormenting anyone around them, including their own parents. *Especially* their parents."

Sugressa crossed her arms. "You're such a sourpuss, Fecanya."

"Yeah, I'm horrible." She started away. "If you insist on coming with me, I can't guarantee I'll be fun company."

Sugressa bounced her shoulders again and waved goodbye. "I'll be ready!"

Out of Ordure

Chapter Thirteen

It's so beautiful out here!" Sugressa gazed at the boulder-strewn hills and mountains, just turning golden-red as the eastern sun broke over the horizon.

"You've already said that," Fecanya replied. "Four times." She glanced at the other fairy, who was practically dancing as they walked. "Actually, you've been going on about it since we stepped out of the portal. Half an hour ago."

"How can you not see the beauty that surrounds us, Fecanya?" Sugressa spread her arms and leaned her head back, letting the sun wash over her face.

"I see dirt, clay, cacti, and venomous life forms. And it's hot."

Sugressa put her hands on her hips and frowned at her. "You're such a grumpy-pants."

"I'm wearing a dress."

"Made of potato bag material."

"Burlap. More stout."

The Sugar Fairy tilted her head. It looked like a goblin working on a math problem. If goblins were pretty, anyway. "I don't think I've ever met a fairy that dresses like that."

"You ever met one in my line of work?"

"Not really. The last Ordure Engineers mostly stayed to themselves." She tapped her cheek. "I don't even think I knew their names, come to think of it."

Fecanya snorted. "Take my word for it. City shit fairies aren't too sociable."

"But why wouldn't they be? Every job is important."

Fecanya stared incredulously at the Sugar Fairy's innocent expression. It was actually an honest question. "Well ... you tend to want more alone time when you work this job."

"Dunghilda was nice."

Fecanya nodded. "Dunghilda was a country Shit Fairy. Big difference."

"There is?" Sugressa frowned. "How so?"

"I'm not going into the specifics, but let's just say that processing manure out in the country is a lot less undesirable than doing it in the city. Not as many primates."

It wasn't until they started uphill, that Sugressa noticed they weren't flying. "Why are we walking?"

"Fresh air," Fecanya said, wiping sweat from her forehead.

"But shouldn't we get to the treatment plant as soon as possible."

"You work a job like this long enough, you take the fresh air moments when you can, and enjoy them as long as you can."

They walked on in silence while Sugressa enjoyed the sunrise, and all the local desert denizens scurrying and slithering along the ground. Somewhere in one of the few sweltering trees in the city, a bird chirped. A louder answering chirp came from several yards away. The contest continued to headache proportions until a third bird chirped what must have been the equivalent of "shut up."

Sugressa fidgeted. How someone could fidget while walking, Fecanya couldn't guess, but fidget she did. "What is it, Sugar Girl?"

"Sugar Girl?"

"It's better than Cloy."

"Or you could use my name."

"I like nicknames."

"Oh?" Sugressa smiled at her. "What should I call you?"

"Annoyed."

"Oh Fecanya."

They started up yet another incline in the rocky terrain. "I know you're enjoying this oven-like air and all, but might we just get there and get our job done? We can always relax afterwards. Maybe even make a picnic!"

To her own surprise, Fecanya didn't openly mock the idea. Maybe because she knew it would hurt the bubbly girl's feelings, and she kinda liked Sugressa. Kinda. "Yeah well, we'll see," she mumbled. "Let's go."

The two fairies spread their wings and buzzed into the air. Once they got their bearings and spotted the treatment facility, they made straight for it. Sugressa gave Fecanya a sly grin, then zoomed ahead.

Fecanya sped up and grinned at her, then dropped low to the ground, zipping around trees and mounds, cacti and boulders. Sugressa whizzed ahead again, and Fecanya found herself actually having fun. *It's all that damn sugar she spreads. Must be spilling out of her pores and infecting me.* She chuckled in spite of herself.

All too soon they reached the treatment facility, and the two fairies hid behind a wide cactus a hundred yards away.

Sugressa pinched her nose. "I wish I knew if there were any animals in there we could mimic. It'd be a lot easier than having to sneak around invisible."

Fecanya held her hand cupped over her mouth. "Dogs have a sense of smell that is many times stronger than a human's, and they don't have oxygen filter masks. Trust me, no animal is within a mile of this place. It was true. There wasn't a single form of life capable of locomotion anywhere in sight.

"And I don't plan on staying around long enough to get tired holding an invisibility charm anyway. We'll get in, snoop around, maybe overhear a conversation, then get out."

"Fine by me," Sugressa nasaled. "Lead on."

*　　　*　　　*

They remained low to the ground as they glided toward the facility, finally calling upon their innate magic to go invisible once they were near.

They lifted back into the air and passed over giant circular vats with flat arms rotating slow and constant. Fecanya studiously ignored them, but beside her Sugressa made a tiny gurgling sound. "Don't think about it," she warned the girl. "In and out. We won't be long."

"I'm trying," Sugressa's disembodied voice said next to her. "It's just so hard to believe ..."

"Don't ... think about it."

Thankfully, they moved beyond the churning vats and into the control section of the facility. They hovered in place, searching for any sign of what a knowledgeable human looked like.

"I don't think we're going to find anyone from up here," Sugressa said.

Fecanya snapped her fingers, and her iBerry phone appeared. "Don't know why I didn't think of this before."

"Oh goodness!" Sugressa squeaked. "Not that thing again! Human technology, Fecanya?"

"Oh relax, Cloy. This'll speed things up."

"*Please* stop calling me Cloy."

Fecanya tapped an icon on the screen that looked like a large primate walking on feet and knuckles, and wearing suit.

"I don't get it," Sugressa said.

The disembodied voice over her shoulder startled Fecanya, and she almost dropped her phone. "Will you kindly not do that? And I thought you didn't like human technology."

"That doesn't mean I don't find it interesting," Sugressa replied, "if dangerous."

"Eh. Whatever." Fecanya logged into the Device Locator app. "This can find the phone of the person we're looking for."

"Why does it have a picture of a well-dressed ape?"

Fecanya frowned. "Well, I modified the icon to look more appropriate for the app's purpose."

"A well-dressed ape?"

"What else would you call a human?" She typed Dr. Carlisle's name into the phone, then snapped her fingers. Little sparks of magic shone from her fingers, and the little loading icon started rotating. After a few moments, the doctor's phone came up on her GPS.

"Perfect! We go that way." She pointed west. "Not a bad guess. We were almost on top of him."

"That's all nice, Fecanya," Sugressa said. "But could you tell me where to go? I can't see you."

"Ah." Fecanya made her hand visible and pointed. "There."

They made their way down to the top floor of the treatment plant, and landed at the top of a flight of metal stairs. "Hold on a second." Fecanya moved her hand in a simple gesture, pressed a thumb and forefinger together and made a zipping motion across her mouth, then Sugressa's. She ended the spell with a snap of her fingers. "Alright, now we can talk without being heard."

"Brilliant," Sugressa said, and Fecanya could practically hear the smile in the other fairy's voice.

They descended the metal stairs and skulked along the halls, Fecanya occasionally consulting her phone's GPS as she led them through the maze of hallways and tech rooms.

"This place is massive, Sugressa breathed. How do they build such things without magic?"

"This is nothing," Fecanya said. "You should see some of their other structures. They may be sloppy and destructive, but they know how to build stuff. Hold on a second." She performed another gesture with her hands, and snapped her fingers. They suddenly heard the voice of a man giving a presentation somewhere in a room further down.

Just for an instant, Fecanya made her hand visible and reached for Sugressa. "It's easier than having to verbally direct you."

"That voice faded out before I could get a feel for how far away he was," Sugressa said, taking the proffered hand.

"I'll do it again when I feel like we're closer."

"Fecanya, you do know the effect would last longer if you used your wand, right?"

"I know. It also would last longer if I did the full spell, instead of the instant one."

"I still don't understand why you don't use your wand. That's what it's for."

Fecanya thought of the other Fairies' normal twig-like wands and snapped, "Because I just don't want to, okay? I don't like using the thing. I like to keep in practice with my hands."

There was a brief pause of invisible silence. "I'm sorry."

Fecanya sighed. "No. I'm sorry. I didn't mean to bite your head off. It's just … a sensitive subject for me."

"Oh it's okay," Sugressa said, the cheer in her voice returning. "We've all got our thing."

"Yeah. Thing."

They crept through a maze of hallways passing door after door until Fecanya called for another stop. After assessing Dr. Carlisle's location, she led Sugressa further down the hall until they came to a door with muffled conversation coming from the other side.

As Sugressa listened at the door, Fecanya fished out her phone and fired up the location app. "Yup. This is the spot."

"I could have told you that," the sugar fairy said. "I can hear him talking."

Fecanya snarled at her. "Well, pardon me for being thorough …"

"Ssh."

Fecanya growled and moved beside Sugressa to press her ear to the door.

"… because as everyone here knows," they heard Dr. Carlisle saying, "the earth's resources are not unlimited. We must find a way to renew and reuse our resources."

Or stop living together in gigantic clumps and suck all the resources dry, Fecanya thought.

"We've made huge leaps with recycling and reusing plastics, everything from making containers and bags, and even clothing. We even have hemp plastic that biodegrades in less than a year."

Dr. Carlisle went silent as he waited for applause to subside. "We recycle the parts from cars, electronic devices, glass …"

"Will you get to it already," Fecanya whispered, "you motor-mouthed monkey-man."

"That's not very nice," Sugressa said.

"Am I supposed to care?"

"Ssh."

"… determined that it would be extremely beneficial to reuse our water. In fact, not only would it be beneficial, but it's absolutely possible."

There was a silent pause and Fecanya waved to Sugressa. "He's probably showing them something."

"On it," Sugressa said. She pulled out her wand and, with a circular gesture leaving a trail of colored mist, tapped the door. The mist settled on an eye level part of the door, and that area faded away.

Oblivious to the magically created spyhole, a man in a white lab coat and shirt, with brown slacks and goggles atop his head, operated a projector.

Fecanya watched as one image after another lit the screen.

"And here," Dr. Carlisle continued, "you can see the progression of water treatment, which we've been doing for thousands of years. Simply boiling water to purify it is in fact, water treatment. There are already countries that utilize treated sewage water for every task, including drinking water."

Fecanya looked at the spot where Sugressa was no doubt crouched next to her.

"Do you look as disgusted as I feel?" she heard Sugressa ask.

"Probably worse," Fecanya replied.

"Now judging from some of the guardedly hesitant looks I'm seeing here," Carlisle said. "I'm sure many of you are imagining microbes and all manner of impurities slipping through the proverbial "cracks" in treatment. Not to mention the very idea of drinking treated wastewater."

"Shit water," Fecanya corrected.

"But I assure you, this technology already exists, and has been around for years. What Carlisle Industries has done," he clicked to the next image, "is expand on this technology. Not only will we convert any form of wastewater into water suitable for bathing, drinking, etcetera, but we will do it on a massive scale. We've spent the last ten years building this mega treatment facility right here in Garmon City."

Fecanya watched the human saunter over to the side of the projector screen to a machine that looked like a large coffeemaker.

"This right here," Carlisle said, patting the top of the machine, "is a micro-treatment unit. Despite its size, it can treat the water of an entire household for a year." He placed a cup under a spout in the front.

"No," Fecanya said. "No no no no no. No."

"He's not going to drink that," Sugressa said hesitantly.

Dr. Carlisle downed the contents of the cup in one gulp, to the chuckling, muttering, and applause of the attendees. He spread his hands. "As you can see, I'm not turning green in the face …"

"But I am," Fecanya said.

"… and am quite fine. The water tastes just like any other water, as far as water taste goes." More chuckling. "Not only has this water been treated of ninety-nine point nine-nine percent of all impurities, but the machine also infuses it with more oxygen. We can service all of Garmon City with one mega plant, and as the technology evolves, one facility could service larger areas."

"That's it," Fecanya turned and leaned her back against the door. "I don't want to live on this planet anymore."

She heard the sound of giggling coming from everywhere and nowhere. Fecanya froze, and looked down each end of the hallway. More giggling. She felt a chill creep down her spine.

"They're coming out," Sugressa said.

Fecanya straightened and pointed down the hall. "Let's go!" No response. "Oh, right. Back the way we came."

Once at the top level of the facility again, the fairies became visible to one another and zipped into the air.

"Can we stop for a minute?" Sugressa panted. "Please?"

Fecanya grudgingly angled toward the ground, and they touched down a mile from the plant.

Sugressa looked over her shoulder in the direction of the now distant facility. "Were we fleeing something I wasn't aware of?"

"Yeah," Fecanya replied. "Human stupidity."

"It's not a bad idea, you know," Sugressa said.

Fecanya shook her head. "Look, they can eat or drink whatever they want. They could take to drinking mud and calling it smoothies, for all I care, so long as I don't have to do it."

"Then why the urgency?"

"The scale of what that primate is talking about," Fecanya said. "If something goes wrong …"

"What could go wrong, Fecanya?" Sugressa asked. "It's not like it's a bomb they're building."

The image in her mind of a giant shit bomb falling from the sky was enough to send Fecanya tunneling underground with the dwarves and goblins. She thought about that ominous giggling back in the facility and felt another chill.

"Call it a hunch. We need to get out of here."

Out of Ordure

Chapter Fourteen

Twelve bottles of antibacterial hand wash. Check. Twenty bottles of antibacterial hand sanitizer. Check. Forty bottles of antibacterial lotion. Check. Knee-high rubber boot sloggers, just in case. Check."

Hands on hips, Fecanya inventoried each of her possessions, then sent them levitating into her stylish burlap extradimensional tote. She glanced over at the polished marble table and tea set. "Not leaving this for them to auction off." She snapped her fingers. The tea set floated over and dropped into her tote as the table lifted into the air, shrank to a fraction of its former size, and dropped in as well.

She dropped the table into her tote with the last of over a hundred items, then closed the bag.

Fecanya grinned as she double-checked her things. All was in order, her important belongings accounted for, and her letter of resignation ready to shoot through the mail slot and onto Deliah Harmass's desk as soon as she glided out of her pod. A tiny part of her would miss Sugressa. Although the chipper Sugar Fairy got on her nerves with all the bright "happy fun-time, life's an endless joy" BS that made Fecanya nauseous, she was still something like a friend.

She thought of Garbita and Bloomara, and grudgingly admitted to herself that she might even miss them. A little. "Eh. They're not so bad, I guess," Fecanya grumbled. "Just doing their job, like anyone else. They just do it like they've got an extra bit of pixie dust rammed up their ..."

She heard a muffled knock on the tinted film of her pod, and turned to see Sugressa, wings beating to keep her hovering in place. "May I come in, Fecanya?" came the muffled request.

Fecanya waved her hand in a circle. The film faded away, and Sugressa glided through. Fecanya waved her hand again, and the film returned, dimming the outside noise of constant work in the Rotunda.

Sugressa's orange eyes turned this way and that, as she looked over the empty pod. "Where are all your furnishings, Fecanya?"

"I'm making a move toward minimalism." She deflated under the sugar fairy's scrutiny. "Alright look, I'm outta here, okay? It's time to go."

Sugressa blinked. "But why?"

"*But why?*" Fecanya squeaked, then immediately regretted it. "Sorry." She gave the girl an awkward pat on the shoulder. "It's a bad habit." She spread her hands to indicate nothing in particular. "I'm sure everyone here is pretty happy with their setup. You get to sweeten things. Everybody likes sweet stuff. Bloom makes flowers happy, which makes bees happy, which makes everyone else happy. Especially when you don't have a stinger in the ass."

"I'm not sure I follow," Sugressa replied.

Fecanya blinked. "Oh, right. Well, look, I'm outta here. Processing everyone's ... leavings, is bad enough, but I've dealt with it. I also have to think about my future, here. I gotta be proactive." She pointed in the direction of the wastewater mega processing plant. "Humans have a knack for overestimating themselves."

"It's a fantastic idea," Sugressa said.

"It's a disaster waiting to happen."

"Why are you so negative?"

Fecanya snorted. "Monkey-boy thinks his facility can purify crap-water at a constant rate of a few minutes per metric ton, and power the entire city while providing drinking water in the deal? Nope. Those machines are gonna crap out in the worst way imaginable. Pun intended." She didn't mention that giggling she'd heard. *Hope I'm not going crazy.*

Sugressa listened patiently through the rant. "But if that were to happen, we'd need you more than ever."

Fecanya nodded her head vigorously. "Eg-*friggin*-xactly! That's why I'm packing up and getting as far from here as possible. When that plant geysers shit a thousand feet into the air and bathes all of Garmon City in it, I'll be on an island somewhere, with sand between my toes, sipping on a foofy drink with an umbrella in it. Frozen. Salted rim. Maybe even an orange wheel."

"You can't just bail out, Fecanya," Sugressa said. "What if there's a way to prevent this? What if ..."

"What if you, Bloom, Garbage Girl, and ole Lieutenant Commander Hard-Ass formed a," Fecanya waved her hands in the air, "I dunno. Crap Compost Coalition, or something. You all can clean it up. I'm done. I was perfectly happy working out in the country ..." her mouth twitched. "Okay, maybe not *perfectly* happy, but I was happier processing *fertilizer* out there, than having to do it in this nasty city full of nasty primates and their nasty habits." She pointed over her shoulder. "And when the crap falls from the sky and starts to sizzle on the scorching ground out there, let them deal with it."

"This isn't a nasty city," Sugressa calmly replied. "And most humans are quite civilized."

Fecanya laughed. "Sure, sweetie." She stood in front of the doorway film and waved it open. "Welp, I guess I'll be seeing ya!"

"Fecanya."

"What?"

"You're better than this. You can act as disgruntled as you like, but you're better. You won't just leave when the whole city is on the verge of a catastrophe."

Fecanya held up a finger. *"Au contraire."* She dropped out of the pod and flew toward the nearest exit tunnel.

"I'm not letting you leave so easy," Sugressa said from behind. "You're a lovely fairy, Fecanya. You're kind and considerate underneath all that hostility. You care about all of us. You just don't want us to know. And that's fine. I'll keep your secret."

Fecanya angled left and down, speeding toward an exit tunnel. At the bottom floor of the Rotunda, she saw Davin Gravelchin hammering away at a massive stake in the wall. He gave one last pound, and the stake fell away, along with a sizable chunk of the wall. The dwarf wiped sweat from his brow, and planted the stake in the next spot.

Guess I should say goodbye. Fecanya glided toward the busy dwarf and touched down behind him. "Hey Gravelchin."

Hammer over his head, Davin half turned to regard her. "Hey little sprite." He lowered the hammer and gave her a once-over. "What's with the bag?"

"She's leaving us," Sugressa said from behind.

Fecanya glared over her shoulder at the sugar fairy, who stood with her arms crossed, orange eyes defiant.

Davin raised his bushy eyebrows. "Eh? Yer leavin'? What're ye about, then?"

"Time to move on," Fecanya said. "I just wanted to say goodbye."

The crusty dwarf faced her and took his cap in his hands. Fecanya hopped back to avoid her feet being coated in the dirt and grit falling out of the cap.

"Ain't gonna be the same with ye gone," Davin said. "Guess I can't blame ye, what with yer profession and all, pardon me frankness."

Fecanya opened and closed her mouth. "Um, yeah."

Davin Gravelchin twisted his hat back and forth in his giant hands, and Fecanya could hear the tough fabric straining not to tear apart.

"Well, be gone with ye, then," the dwarf said, turning his back. He waved a hand over his shoulder. "I ain't sayin' I'll miss ye, so don't go fishin' fer it!"

Fecanya hurried away to avoid the shrapnel from the stone wall as the dwarf went back to hammering. She and Sugressa lifted into the air and through the exit, navigating the many tunnels lit by the phosphorescent brownies who continuously swept and cleaned the rocky passages.

A cloudless night greeted them at the end of the tunnel, along with one other thing …

Fecanya groaned at the sight of a shrouded figure standing at the mouth of the exit, fists on hips, and a big round thing on top of her head that could be nothing other than a bun. Not even Garbita's bun was so formidable.

"And where do you think you're going?" Bloomara demanded.

Out of Ordure

Chapter Fifteen

Fecanya and her uninvited companion came to a stop in front of the Bloom Fairy, who frowned at them both.

"I might have expected such behavior from you, Fecanya," Bloomara said. "But you." She turned her icy gaze over Sugressa, who shrank away. "I would expect better."

"I'm ... sorry, Bloomara," the sugar fairy said.

"She's not trying leave with me," Fecanya said, and Sugressa's face lit with appreciation. "She was trying to keep me from leaving."

"Which brings us back to my original question. Where do you think you're going?"

"*Who*, exactly do you think you are?" Fecanya countered. "Last I heard, we're not indentured servants in this place. Am I supposed to check in with you before I do something?"

"Abandoning your job would fall into something that must pass by me, yes."

"Who told you I was abandoning anything?" Fecanya asked.

Bloomara's gray eyes glittered when she leaned forward. "You did."

"I did no such thing ..." She stopped at the sound of Sugressa clearing her throat. "What?"

"Um ... actually you did. When you said I was trying to stop you. That kinda means you were leaving."

Fecanya closed her eyes.

"Must I repeat my question a third time?" Bloomara asked.

"I need a break," Fecanya replied, eyes still closed.

"That requires you to sneak away in the middle of the night?"

"Look, Bloom. I promise I'll return." *In about sixty or seventy years, for about an hour.*

"You must think me a fool to believe that," Bloomara said. "Do you not know that we keep track of our staff? Do you think your visits with Dr. Leowitriss are undocumented or reviewed?"

Fecanya ground her teeth. *What did that furry-legged prude tell them?*

Bloomara grinned as if reading her mind. "Ironically, it was your report that gave you away. An unstable wastewater mega plant that could leave the entire city drenched in filth. Filth that you would have to deal with."

"Yeah," Fecanya said, shoulders drooping. "Filth."

"Deliah called myself and Dr. Leowitriss into her office as soon as she read yours and Sugressa's report, and we agreed that this situation might be a tipping point for you." She spread her arms. "And so here I am."

"Violating my civil rights."

Bloomara's arms dropped. "Your what?"

"You not letting me leave is violating my civil rights. I have a right to leave."

"Your civil what?" Bloomara curled her fingers into fists at her side. "We are not humans who think to step outside our place in the world. Every living being has its place and its function."

"So that's it then," Fecanya said. "I'm born an Ordure Engineer for all my existence. I have to process crap, like, forever. That's it?"

"You are not the only Ordure Engineer in the world, Fecanya."

"Then bring some of them in to deal with this. I'm ready to retire."

"To retire?" Bloomara put her fists on her hips. "Now you listen to me ..."

Ugh. She's losing her patience.

"Your attitude has been tolerated thus far because of your abrupt reassignment to Garmin City from the countryside. I know it's been an adjustment, but you have a job to do." Bloomara's visage softened. "And if you must know, you're the most capable to handle this. Deliah has put out a call for other Ordure Engineers to assist, should the problem escalate."

"What was the response?" Sugressa asked.

Bloomara glanced at the sugar fairy, likely having forgotten she was there.

"If ... if you must know, the response was rather ... lackluster."

Can't see why. Who wouldn't want to process frying dung in the scorching desert heat. "I see."

"Fecanya. You know I cannot forcibly detain you, but I would have you know that we ... we need you. Even without this potential disaster looming over our heads, your presence has greatly benefitted Garmon City. Despite your attitude and insufferable antics at times, you are an asset. And without you, we can't contain that mega facility."

"Wow," Fecanya said. "It must be twisting your insides to say all that." She nearly giggled when Bloomara growled. "Tell ya what; I'll just take a little vacation for, oh, maybe five or six years. Maybe ten. When I return, if the facility blows its top, I'll be here to do my job."

"You know very well that if something is going to happen, it will be before then," Bloomara growled. "Likely in the next few days."

Fecanya offered her best innocent expression. "We don't know that for sure."

Bloomara took a deep breath. "Look. I'm sure it's tickling your black heart that I'm standing here asking you to help us. Believe me, there are many things I'd rather do ..."

"Like wait till the mega plant blows and clean up the fallout?" Fecanya interrupted.

Another deep breath. "Have it your way. I'll just ask that if you have even a spec of basic fairy decency, consider all of those who would be affected."

As much as Fecanya wanted to deny it, the Bloom Fairy's words made a dent in her armor. "Oh fine, okay? Fine. I'll think about it."

Bloomara clasped her hands together. "Good. Good." She stood there, grinning.

Fecanya stood there, grinning.

Everyone stood there, grinning.

"Um ... so you gonna get outta my way?"

"Hm?"

"Are you," Fecanya pointed at her, "going to step aside?" She pointed at the side of the tunnel exit.

"Oh." Bloomara's mouth opened and closed a few times as she worked up a response. "I ... I thought you said ..."

"That I'd think about it. I didn't say I'd think about it here." She shouldered past, not bothering to see if Sugressa was following, but knowing she would. "Been good talking to you, Bloom. And I appreciate the grudging vote of confidence."

"When will we know your decision?" Bloomara asked from behind.

With half her thoughts on a tropical island somewhere, Fecanya could only shrug. "If the city turns in to one huge biohazard dump and I'm nowhere to be seen, take it as my deciding to retire."

Before her supervisor could respond, she spread her wings and flew into the night sky.

Chapter Sixteen

While birds and small primates called to each other in the nearby jungle, cicadas maintained their constant buzz that could only be enjoyable to other cicadas. A breeze blew in off the ocean and caressed the two fairies, who lounged in the shade of a leaning coconut tree.

The former Ordure Engineer stirred the little umbrella in her frozen drink with thumb and forefinger, pinky finger raised. "Ah ghant b'leeve Ah haven't qhwit ah lhong time agho," Fecanya slurred. "Dhon't know why Ah been prhocessin' shite me whole lhife when Ah could be lhivin' it up heer."

Sugressa carefully lifted her giant hurricane glass, and sipped her piña colada, gazing out at the rippling waves. They rose into the air and, with a primal roar, fell upon the beach, sliding down the white sands like lust filled fingers. "Mhmm."

Fecanya swiveled her head around much like an infant, and looked at the sugar fairy. "Why'd you come heer with me, aghain?"

Sugressa took another sip. "The fact that you've nearly finished an entire pint of alcoholic beverage should be answer enough. You really need to be careful. You can't drink like a human, you know."

Fecanya flopped her hand at Sugressa in a dismissive gesture. "Oh dhon't bhee so shtuffy. What else we have to dho? If you can't enjhoy yourself, Shugressa, you need to gho home. You're khillin' me bhuzz."

Sugressa took another careful sip. "I'm just looking out for you, that's all. It's what friends do."

Fecanya gave her what was supposed to be a skeptical look, but came off as a squint. "Hmph. You're supphosed to be the fhun one, Shugressa." She flopped her hand out to encompass the tiny uninhabited island. "I'd expect Gharbita or Blhoomara to be all shtuffy out heer, but nhot you. It's so nice heer. No shite-hurlin' mhonkeysh, no prosheshin mhonkey shite, no ..." she looked around the deserted tropical island, at their only companion, an iguana, lounging in the shade beside them. "No shite. There's no shite anywhere, Shugressa. No shite at all." She started to sob.

Sugressa started to reach for the other fairy, hesitated, then leaned over and gave Fecanya an awkward pat on her bouncing shoulders. "There there, Fecanya. It's okay."

Fecanya sniffed. "I jush ... there's no shite, Shugressa. I don't have to clean up any shite. And if there was any laying around heer, like from that shnake ..."

"It's an iguana."

"... I shtill wouldn't have to proshesh it up."

"I know, lovely girl. I'm sure it's nice not to have to do that."

Fecanya looked at the sugar fairy, tears streaming down her cheeks. "I love you, Shugressa. You know that?" She flopped her hand over her shoulder. "You and Linda."

"Oh ... stop it," Sugressa responded shyly, still patting her on the shoulder. "And will you stop calling that iguana Linda? It's an iguana."

"No, I mean it," Fecanya said. "You're like that annoying little shishter that keepsh things all nice and ... and ... and sweet, you know? That's why ever'bhody likes you,

Shugressa. You're all … nice and shweet. Like a sack of shugar, or shomething."

Sugressa responded with a crinkled smile. "Um … well thank you. I … love you too."

"Aaaaaw." Fecanya lunged in and wrapped Sugressa in a tight hug, sloshing some of the frozen contents of her glass onto the sugar fairy's leg.

Sugressa let out a little yelp at the cold, and Fecanya gasped.

"Oh no! I friggin' shpilt on you! Let me clean that." She proceeded to smear the frozen margarita up and down her leg, while Sugressa bit her lip against the freezing cold.

"That's, quite enough," she gasped. "I'll be fine, thank you." She pried Fecanya's hand away, and snapped her fingers, producing a little handkerchief.

"How lhong you gonna shtick heer with me?"

Sugressa finished cleaning her leg, and balled up the handkerchief. She tossed it into the air and snapped her fingers, and the cloth disappeared in a little spark of glittering dust. "How long are *you* planning to stay here Miss Fecanya?"

The inebriated fairy straightened her back and shook her head side to side. "Miss Fecanya. Don't you gho talkin' like that shtuffy Leowitlessh, now. Ah can't shtand for it. And Ah told you. I'm retired."

Sugressa started to take another sip of her piña colada, but stopped when her head felt a little fuzzy. "I don't know why I grabbed a full pint of this. Even half would kill me." She looked at Fecanya's glass and almost fell over. "You've almost finished yours. Put that down." She grabbed the drink out of Fecanya's hand.

"Hey. Ghive it back."

Sugressa held the other fairy at bay, fending off the reaching hands like one would the efforts of an invertebrate out of water. "You've had enough, Fecanya."

They stopped struggling at the sound of James Brown's *Super Bad*, and Fecanya reached into the pocket of her capris and pulled out her phone.

"How do you get reception out here?" Sugressa asked. She looked around. "We're nowhere near a human civilization."

Fecanya rolled her eyes at the other fairy. "The shame way we magicked our way behind that bar in Hawaii, shnatched our drinksh, and magicked our way heer. Magic!" After a few swipes and taps, Fecanya opened her news app.

"What's it say?" Sugressa asked, leaning over to have a look.

Fecanya turned away. "Nothing." She tried to shove her phone back into her pocket, but Sugressa was quicker, and more sober. "Hey! Ghive that back." She tried to grab her phone, but her arms just waved independently of her will.

Sugressa took in a long, ominous breath. "Oh my."

Chapter Seventeen

W ill you let me gho?" Fecanya growled, pulling against Sugressa's firm grip on her wrist.

"You're coming back with me," the Sugar Fairy said.

"I am *not*." Fecanya continued to pull away, but it was like her wrist was in a vice. How'd this sugar runt get so strong?

"I'm not letting you sit here in this paradise while a catastrophe happens," Sugressa said. She pulled Fecanya away from the heavenly shade of the coconut tree, and away from their local buddy, Linda. The iguana lazily turned her head to regard them, but otherwise made no other movement.

"I'm not going to let you lounge here now, and regret it later."

"I ain't reghrettin' nothin'," Fecanya slurred.

"I know you don't, right now," Sugressa replied, muscling her along. She stopped and waved her hand in a circle. Little glittering sparks winked in and out to form a slit in the air in front of them. The slit rotated, then opened into a three-foot-tall portal.

"No!" Fecanya pulled and tugged, but her legs and arms were still like tentacles made of jelly, and Sugressa easily yanked her along. "Bye, Lhinda!" the drunken fairy yelled just before they disappeared into the portal.

Linda blinked her left eye and worked her mouth open and closed a couple times, then looked back to the beach.

*   *   *

"Oomph!" Fecanya glared up at Sugressa from the ground. As soon as they were back in the tunnels of Fae World Maintenance Services, the sugar fairy had released her. "You could have given a little warning before you let me go."

Without a word, Sugressa waved her hands in the space in front of Fecanya, then snapped her fingers.

Fecanya sat on her sore rump and sighed in resignation as the fuzzy bliss brought on by that delicious margarita slowly faded away. When the cotton cleared out of her head, she stood and swiped her hands down her blouse and capris with as much dignity as she could manage. She spared a glare at Sugressa and snapped her fingers. Her flowery blouse and capris became her usual knee-length burlap dress.

"Why do you insist on wearing that dull garment," Sugressa asked. "You looked so cute in your other outfit. You can wear more interesting clothes at work, you know?"

"Yeah thanks for that," Fecanya said, walking past. "In my line of work, you tend not to want to wear anything nice." She reached into her extradimensional travel bag, and withdrew a sweet bark cigarette.

"You don't touch any of that dirty stuff, Fecanya."

Dirty stuff. "All the same." She lit the cigarette, took a long, blissful draw, and stomped down the tunnel.

Sugressa trotted after her. "You seem angry."

To her distress, Fecanya found herself touched at Sugressa's worried tone. She was genuinely concerned that Fecanya would be mad at her. "Yeah I'm angry. Angry at myself for not deleting that app on my phone when I 'retired.'"

"If I remember how those things work, they can also tune in to human news channels. You would have seen the news sooner or later, and you would have regretted it."

"Whatever."

Sugressa smiled at her.

Fecanya blew out a purple cloud of smoke, and gave Sugressa a sidelong look. *What the hell is she grinning at?*

They continued through the snaking tunnel, the green and yellow lights from the tiny brownie workers lost on Fecanya as she marched toward the center of the complex.

"You know," Sugressa said. "After this whole mess is taken care of, you could just ask for a proper vacation. I'm sure Deliah would … OH!" They rounded a corner and came face to face with Leowitriss. Or rather, Sugressa came face to knee.

The sugar fairy hit the ground with a thud, and raised up on an elbow, pressing a hand to her forehead.

"Oh my!" The satyr bent and helped her to her feet. "My deepest apologies. Are you alright, Miss …"

"Sugressa. My name is Sugressa, and I'm fine, thank you."

"Way to go, Leo," Fecanya said. She tossed her nearly finished cigarette into the air, and snapped her fingers. It disappeared in a purple puff. "You just can't control those sexy, furry knees." She inspected Sugressa's forehead. "That's probably going to leave a knot." She looked up at the therapist, who looked concerned. "I know you folk like it rough, but not everyone …"

"That is *quite* enough, Miss Fecanya," Leowitriss snapped. "Is it so difficult for you to maintain some semblance of decency?"

"Some semlbaunce of decenceh," Fecanya mocked. "You really need to loosen up, Leo."

"My *name*, is …"

"Leowitless, I know, I know."

The satyr gnashed his teeth. "You're sure you're alright, Miss Sugressa?"

Hand still pressed to her forehead, Sugressa nodded. "I'm fine. Thank you, sir."

Leowitriss nodded. "Please. Call me Leowitriss. If you've ever a need for counseling, feel free to come see me." He adjusted his spectacles on the bridge of his nose and smiled. "Good day to you." His smile reversed when he looked at Fecanya. "Miss Fecanya.

"Later, Leo … *witriss.*"

"Why do you give him such a hard time?" Sugressa asked, after the therapist—practically running—was out of sight.

"He takes pleasure in listing all my faults, reading them item by item from his thick binder that is my file."

"Isn't that part of his job?" Sugressa asked. "To show you where you can improve, and help you get there?"

"Maybe. But I doubt doing it in such a haughty manner is part of the job description. The first day I walked into his office, he looked me up and down, wrinkled his nose, and just started reading my file out loud. He even wiped the chair I was sitting in when I got up." Fecanya sniffed. "Besides, you can't tell me you've ever seen a stuffier satyr. How can I not have fun with that? How he became a therapist, I can't imagine. He's a big snob that's easily riled."

Despite the knot swelling on her forehead, Sugressa giggled. "Maybe so, but you really should go easy on him. He's not such a bad guy."

"Eh, whatever."

Sugressa looked down the tunnel. "He seemed like he was in a hurry."

"Probably late for high tea."

They heard the buzz of activity long before they reached the Rotunda. Gravelly voices yelled instructions through a cacophony of arguing and tools striking solid earth.

"That sounds like dwarves," Sugressa said.

"Dwarves and goblins," Fecanya replied. "Something's up."

When they finally did reach the Rotunda, both fairies stopped and took in the chaos. Dwarves and goblins ran to and fro, oftentimes the former knocking the latter over in the rush.

"What the hell is going on?" Fecanya said, flinching as an unwitting goblin stepped in front of a running dwarf. The dwarf tried to stop, but bringing a wedge of solid muscle to a sudden halt isn't easy. Both went down in a tumble of limbs, beard, and floppy ears.

"Gyat durned stinkin …" the dwarf hopped to his feet. "If ye can't be seein' where yer goin', best clip them durned flaps o' cartilage away from yer face, or I'm fer stompin' right over ye next time."

"Ain't my fault," the goblin squeaked in response, once the dwarf was safely out of earshot. "Cut that mangy beard and you won't trip over it."

Fairies from every division darted this way and that, some directing workers, others not sure what to do and just flying from place to place, looking busy.

Fecanya and Sugressa walked to the rail and peered over the side. At the bottom floor of the Rotunda, dwarves and goblins were running in and out of tunnels, shouting orders to seal them at the ends, then once that was finished, they sealed them at the Rotunda end. Gnomes flitted between them, applying sealants and moving materials into place for their larger coworkers to use. It was coordinated chaos.

Sugressa frantically waved down a swarm of brownies. "Hey, what's going on?"

The tiny cleaner sprites flowed over to stop in front of the fairies, rippling in the air like an ocean wave. They swirled and buzzed, finally organizing themselves into a triangular shape with an open top. They continued to shift until the triangle filled out.

Sugressa frowned. "A mountain?"

The brownies held the shape, then a number of them zipped out of the top of the mountain shape, spreading out to the left and right.

"Oh. A volcano. That's an eruption!" Sugressa clapped her hands. "This is fun!"

The brownies that formed the lava that burst out of the volcano, swirled in front of it, then formed another shape.

Fecanya looked at the new image and sighed.

Sugressa tilted her head to the side. "What's that? Looks like some kind of ..."

"Turd, Sugressa." Fecanya waved an impatient hand. "It's a turd, okay?"

"A volcano is spewing turds?"

Fecanya turned a dumbfounded expression on the other fairy. The brownies changed shape and formed into a giant head that slowly turned to look at Sugressa with a similar expression.

"OH. I get it!" Sugressa almost hopped. "The mega wastewater plant is spewing turds!"

Fecanya would have laughed if she wasn't about to cry.

"Thanks, guys," Sugressa said, and the head-shaped swarm of brownies nodded in response, and disbursed into the air. She turned to Fecanya. "We'd better find Bloomara."

Fecanya looked over her shoulder in memory of that lovely vacation.

Chapter Eighteen

Fecanya barely recognized Bloomara when they finally found her. The supervisor slid several stray blue locks away from her face as she directed the frantic workers. "No!" she yelled. "Mud will not be enough to stop it. If a flood is strong enough to break through the outside seal, do you truly think a mud stack would stop it? We'd be drowned in filth."

"She looks busy," Fecanya said. "I don't think we should disturb her."

"Bloomara!" Sugressa called.

The blue-haired fairy looked around until she spotted them, and her shoulders rose and fell with what could have been relief. She pulled a larger than normal goblin aside by the elbow. "Jackson. Keep things moving until I return."

"You's gots it, Bleumara," came the yellow-toothed response.

"Is that wise?" Sugressa asked when Bloomara reached them. She looked past her at the knobby-kneed goblin, waving his arms about as he gurgled instructions.

"Jackson is the smartest goblin I've ever met. He'll keep things going until I get back, as long as nothing complicated happens."

"Like counting to five," Fecanya muttered. Bloomara's responding tired expression caught her off guard. "Um. What's going on?"

"What isn't?" Boomer replied. "I sent Garbita with a small team of fairies to keep tabs on the mega plant, and it's now on high alert. The humans are scrambling, as the gauges are going into the red. The volume is too much for their machines to handle, despite their confidence in their state of the art equipment."

Fecanya felt a stab of guilt that a team of fairies were monitoring a waste treatment facility without her. She tried to shrug it off. She needed a break, anyway. When was the last time she'd had one?

"I'm so glad you've returned, Fecanya," Bloomara went on. "We need you."

That caught her by surprise. "You … um. Yeah. I'll do my best."

"Please, we need you out at that mega plant immediately. If it blows, the entire city of Garmin will be covered filth."

"That's one way to put it."

Sugressa turned toward her, but Fecanya held up her hand before the sugar fairy could speak. "Yeah yeah, I know. Save your breath and let's just go. I'm already changing my mind."

No sooner had the words left her mouth than Bloomara pulled out her wand—that Fecanya glanced regretfully at—and created a portal. "You'll find Garbita when you step through."

Fecanya thought of the disembodied giggling she'd heard the last time they were there, along with the sudden unreliability of the machinery at that plant. "Looking forward to it."

*   *   *

Garbita rounded on them as soon as they stepped through, wand pointed in an attack gesture.

20

"Whoa, whoa, Garbage Girl." Fecanya held up her hands. "What's your problem?"

"I *told* you to stop calling me that! I'm a Detritus Redis ... oh bother. Look, we have a huge problem." She pointed over her shoulder. "There are four wastewater treatment plants connected to this mega plant."

"Connected?" Fecanya and Sugressa echoed at the same time.

Fecanya looked past her at the massive facility. "How is that even possible? There are miles between each facility."

"They're connected via underground pipelines," Garbita explained. "Each facility has pipelines that send the liquid leavings to this central point."

"Then why don't they just stop sending it here?" Sugressa asked. "Wouldn't that make sense? They could figure out the problem before it gets worse."

"Because a malfunction has happened at all four of the facilities," Garbita said. "And they're sending *all* of the material here. It's overloading the place."

"So what you're saying," Fecanya replied, "is that this place is going to go supernova."

"That's the general idea, yes."

"Then why are we standing here, instead of someplace a thousand miles away?"

"My girls are at each of the plants working to quell the problems," Garbita said, ignoring her. "Mimily and Siraka are working on the northwest plant, which is the biggest aside from this one. Nell is at the east plant, and Mirisha took the west. Bella took south."

Garbita looked down her rectangular spectacles at them. "It's going to take all of us to stop this catastrophe, so we'd best get moving."

They wove their way between giant vats churning things none of them wanted to think about. Men and women in uniformed shirts, jeans, and hardhats ran to and fro, checking equipment and gauges, filling out reports, and trying not to look panicked.

With all the commotion, the three fairies navigated the chaos easily enough without being noticed.

"Too many humans," Sugressa squealed once they'd reached the central vat.

"I'll make us invisible," Fecanya said, starting the motion.

"Allow me," Garbita said. "With all due *respect*, Fecanya, I'm a little better at it than you. We'll still be able to see each other." She waved her wand in a simple pattern, and one by one they disappeared.

Fecanya was just about to utter a well thought out quip when they each slowly came back into view. Garbita's smug expression made Fecanya wish they were still invisible to each other.

The ground shook, and the three fairies stumbled, then beat their wings to lift themselves off the ground. An alarm sounded, and rotating red lights along the walls lit up and swiped across the facility. Supervisors shouted above the alarms for an immediate evacuation.

"That's definitely not good," Fecanya said. "I'd rather join them."

"We must contain this."

"Yeah I get it. I was just saying what I'd rather do." Fecanya closed her eyes and opened her senses. Almost immediately a wave of nausea fell over her from the right, and she led them that way.

After weaving around stampeding humans and managing not to be trampled, they came to a massive vat that looked like a mountain to the three one-foot-tall fairies.

She heard that faint sound of giggling in the air again. It was the same giggling she'd heard in the alley, then again in rainforest when the Hurlers had launched their biohazard assault. She glanced at the other fairies. Sugressa appeared not to have heard it, but Garbita's eyes nervously darted left and right. She must have been hearing it the whole time she'd been here. Probably why she'd nearly put the whammy on them when they'd first arrived.

"Looks like this is where the biggest problem is," Fecanya said.

"Can you fix it?"

Fecanya shrugged. "The best thing would be to figure out how to shut the thing down."

A portal opened behind them, and out of it stepped Bloomara. "Is there any news? Have you stopped it?"

"No and no," Fecanya said.

"We've found the central problem," Garbita said. "But we must find a way to shut the facility down. The humans are unable to do it, and their equipment is overloaded.

"I can help with that." Bloomara reached into her satchel and produced a glass jar.

"What's in there?" Sugressa asked, lowering her face to the jar.

"A band of Abatwa," Bloomara said. "When I found out about the problem with the facility instruments, I went to one of their colonies in Africa on a hunch we might need them. They're exceptionally handy at getting inside the tiniest places."

"They look so comfortable," Sugressa breathed, as she looked closer. "There must be a hundred in there."

"Two hundred twenty," Bloomara corrected.

"Are they lounging on tiny couches?"

"Couches and hammocks are their favorites. If I was to transport them in a jar, this was the only way they would allow it. Dignity, you understand."

"Of course." Sugressa put her hand beside her face and waved, then squealed in delight when the tiny humanoid figures, legs crossed and arms draped over the back of the sofas, waved back. "They're so *cute!*"

"You can play with them later," Fecanya said. "Good thinking, Bloom. If you can get them to the central computer network that controls this disaster, can they shut it down from the inside?"

"It's one of the things they enjoy doing the most."

107

"Can't say I blame them," Fecanya muttered. "I guess this is it, then. Bloom, we'll try to figure out how to keep this thing from blowing its top while your little guys do their thing."

Bloomara opened her mouth as if she was about to offer some kind of retort, but it ended in a huff. She spun on her heel and ran off.

"What's her problem?" Fecanya asked.

"I think you sort of usurped her authority," Sugressa replied.

Fecanya rolled her eyes. "Whatever." She turned to face the giant vat. "I can feel this thing is overloaded. It's about to burst at the seams."

The ground rumbled again.

"Something about this isn't right," Fecanya said. "The worst that should be happening is that the machinery would just stop working. There's nothing here that should cause tremors."

"I sensed the same thing," Garbita said. "There's more at work here than just a simple machinery failure."

"I don't sense anything," Sugressa said, sounding disappointed.

Garbita gave her a pat on the back. "That's because your talents lie in a different area, girl. Fecanya's and my talents are somewhat … related. As much as I'm loath to admit that."

The ground shook again, this time more violently, and the giggling grew louder.

"Did you hear that?" Sugressa asked.

Fecanya looked at her. Sugressa's face had gone pale. "Yeah I did. You alright?"

"This place scares me all of a sudden," the sugar fairy said.

Fecanya couldn't have agreed more. The giggling grew louder until it filled their heads, and when Fecanya closed her eyes, she saw glaring red eyes staring at her in the darkness.

Chapter Nineteen

N ow I know that sound," Garbita exclaimed. Imps!"
"Imps?" Sugressa said. "You're sure?"
"You wouldn't have much experience with
them," Fecanya said in a strained voice. She looked about,
trying to keep her panic under control. "What's the worst
you've have to deal with at your job, Sugressa? Rubbing a
hive of bees the wrong way?"

"I get along quite nicely with bees, actually."

"The point is, you're less likely to encounter these little
bastards in your line of work. It's not in their nature."

"Oh I get it." Sugressa snapped her fingers. "But because
Garbita's job is trash, and yours ..."

"Right. You got it. Focus."

The pink bun on top of her head bobbed as Sugressa
nodded.

More giggling came from inside the vat.

Garbita's mouth turned down. "I think I'm going to be
sick."

"Me too," Fecanya said, holding her stomach. "Sugressa,
get on my other side."

"What are we going to do?" the sugar fairy asked as she
moved to Fecanya's right side.

"Combine our efforts to keep them from entering this world."

"Entering? But imps live in Dark Faerie. How are they going to come here? Not out of that giant vat?" Sugressa looked like she was ready to bolt.

"Don't you dare move," Fecanya warned. "You dragged me back here. We're seeing this through."

Sugressa patted her bun as she glanced about. "I wasn't going anywhere."

"Sure. Now get ready."

Upon seeing Garbita draw her wand, Sugressa did the same. Fecanya planted her feet, studiously ignoring the other girls watching her.

"An entire flurry of imps will require your wand, Fecanya."

"My wand is available if I need it. Thank you, Garbita." She heard a harrumph from behind.

"I honestly don't know why ..."

"Because I don't need to use it. My wand, my business."

The ground shook again and the giggling grew louder. The three fairies flinched at the buildup of power forming inside the vat. It was growing like a living thing.

"What in Lilith's Underworld is going on in there?" Sugressa asked.

"Imps aren't native to this dimension," Fecanya said. "To enter, they have to use physical matter that's more or less attuned to their nature. Furies and other demon types use violence, war, and even some weapons as a conduit to bring themselves here. In some cases, even a doll."

"A doll?" Sugressa scratched her head. "But dolls are a cute children's toy."

"Dear girl," Garbita said. "Have you ever *seen* some human dolls? They can be positively ghastly."

"So a bunch of imps are using ... that," Sugressa pointed at the vat, "as a conduit to get to this world? Eew." She pressed her fists to her mouth. "Eeeeeeew!"

The ground rumbled again and the giggling reached a fever pitch. Fecanya closed her eyes and extended her awareness. She was instantly assaulted by a wall of malevolent mischief that would have knocked her over, had Garbita and Sugressa not been there to steady her. When she was sure she could stand again, Fecanya lifted her hands, palms facing the vat. "Everyone ready?"

She waved her hands in intricate patterns, moving her fingers, flicking her wrists. Then she rotated her arms in a wide circle and snapped her fingers. A transparent dome appeared over the top of the vat, sparkled for a few moments, then faded.

"What happened?" Garbita asked.

"If they catch a whiff of that dome," Fecanya answered, "they'll try something else. Probably something we're guaranteed not to like. It's there. We just can't see it, and neither can they."

"They're coming through," Garbita said, just before the top of the vat exploded.

The blast was far worse than Fecanya had expected, but her ward held. At present, it looked like a giant black dome sitting atop the broken vat. Thousands of narrow red eyes blinked at them from within the geyser blackness. "That ... is truly disgusting."

"How long will your ward hold?" Garbita asked.

"Given the force of the explosion, and the fact that there's a countless number of the nasty bastards scratching at it, ooooh, mmmmm." Fecanya tapped her cheek. "Minutes? Seconds?"

"Then why are you standing there talking?"

Fecanya snapped her fists at her sides and lunged at the Garbage Fairy. "Because you asked!"

"Um, girls?" Sugressa ventured, pointing at the dome.

Fecanya forcibly straightened her burlap dress while glaring at Garbita. "We need to combine our magic to form a gateway to push them back into Dark Faerie." She stretched her hands out at her sides. Golden fairy fire glowed around her, then the others as they summoned their magic.

Fecanya kept her eyes on the volcanic biohazard. Evil giggling filled her head as the imps tried to break her concentration. "Get out!" She pushed them away, then waved her hands in a circle. Her movements trailed multicolored sparks in the air as the magic gathered and flowed, molded by her will. She closed her eyes, opened herself to the other two, and felt the warmth of their magic filling her.

She drew it in, held it together while focusing on opening a gateway back to Dark Faerie. "Save your energy for when I open that gate. We'll have to keep it open and keep anything on the other side from getting out long enough to shove the imps through."

Sugressa let out a ragged breath. "So many. So much mischief and ill intent. I can barely stand it."

Fecanya felt sympathy for the sugar fairy. It wasn't in her nature to deal with this sort of thing.

She focused on prying open the gateway, and immediately felt a presence. It was as surprised to encounter her as she was to encounter it.

"Ung?" the thing thought. "Ngung!"

What felt like the fattest, slimiest demon Fecanya could imagine turned and lurched toward the newly formed gateway. She got the impression of a demon with a massive belly, short legs, and giant hands connected to long arms. Tiny bat wings flapped on its back with about as much usefulness as arms on a T-Rex.

"Oh no."

"What is it?" Garbita asked. "I feel something there. It's really stupid, but it feels strong."

"It's a knuckle-dragger," Fecanya said. "If that thing gets through, it'll slap us halfway across the state!"

"Oh dear."

She felt Garbita push against the demon, but it laughed at her. "Don't hit it in the belly," Fecanya said. "Hit it in the head."

"There's nothing in its head to damage," Garbita said.

Sweat trickled down Fecanya's face. The combination of the gateway and the hulking knuckle-dragger behind it had sent the imps into a frenzy. The constant giggling had been replaced by shrieking, and they clawed and kicked at the ward, which started to buckle.

"It's got really short legs, Garbita. Hit it in the head and it'll fall backward."

The Detritus Redistributor complied, and whipped her wand in an up and down motion, then brought it around to her side with several circular gestures. She swung her arm forward as though swinging a golf club with one hand.

"Ung!" The fat demon fell backward, stubby legs kicking.

"Now!" Fecanya and Sugressa shoved at the mass of imps, pushing them toward the gate.

The imps fought back, and though they were pushed closer to the gate, they didn't go through.

"Dammit," Fecanya growled.

"Language," Garbita admonished.

"You go ahead and worry about my language," Fecanya replied. "But if those little bastards make it out of there, they'll be everywhere, sabotaging and destroying everything."

Garbita wrinkled her nose. "Will they bring all that conduit material with them?"

"Yup."

Garbita thrust her wand forward, sending a burst of fairy magic punching into the imp mass.

"Hey!" A tiny voice said from inside the dome. "That hurt! Okay, that's it. Step aside."

The mass of evil Fae parted, and a scowling imp floated into view. It grinned at them with sharp teeth and red eyes narrowed into slits. The grin only accentuated the sideways oval shape of its head. "You made a big mistake." The imp made a show of rolling up sleeves it didn't have, then proceeded to flex muscles it also didn't have.

"What's it doing?" Sugressa asked, giggling.

113

The imp launched into a series of flips and spins, clapped its hands together, then started running in place while pushing its fists forward and backward.

"Oh so that's what it's gonna be?" Fecanya twitched her waist left and right as she shuffled forward and backward. Her hands moved in graceful patterns as she continued to feed magic into the dome.

The imp growled, and leapt into a somersault, then hopped onto its toes and spun in a circle.

Fecanya's feet were a blur as she moved forward and backward; one, two, cha-cha-cha. One, two, cha-cha-cha.

The imp fell sideways and spun on its and shoulders, legs spread out as it turned.

"That's impressive," Sugressa breathed, wiping sweat from her forehead.

"A most unrefined form of dance." Garbita sniffed. "*To*tally chaotic."

"Oh don't be such a prude, Garbita. It looks fun."

Garbita's mouth fell open. "You've been hanging about with *her* too long." She jerked her chin at Fecanya.

"Thanks for that," Fecanya said. "I'm really feeling the love, here."

The imp was spinning so fast on its neck and shoulders, it looked like a whirlwind. It curled its legs in and wrapped its arms around them as it started spinning on its back.

Fecanya held the sides of her dress and swished them from one side to the other. She high-stepped and shuffled her feet, turned a circle while holding her hands above her head. She snapped her fingers and a rose appeared in the air, which she clenched in her teeth.

"This is getting ridiculous," Garbita said. "Are you two actually fighting or courting each other?"

Sugressa panted. "I'm running out of steam."

The imp was still spinning on its back, and picking up speed. Dark magic sparked and crackled from its momentum, and the mass of imps still clawing at the dome were strengthened by it.

114

Uh oh. Despite her efforts, the thing was beating her. It had too much speed; too much momentum built up. *Desperate times, desperate measures.* Fecanya stopped her dance, planted her feet, and cupped her hands together. She held her hands at the side of her waist, and half turned away.

"What in the world is that nonsense you're doing?" Garbita asked.

"I can't hold on much longer, Fecanya," Sugressa said. "If you'd just use your wand, you'd have enough power."

Fecanya ignored them. She gathered every bit of magic she had in her. It was more than enough to beat one imp, but she needed a big result. Finally, when she could hold no more, she focused all of it in her hands, leaned forward, and thrust her hands out. "HADOUKEN!"

Out of Ordure

Chapter Twenty

The giant ball of magic flew from her hands and blasted the spinning imp. It screeched as it ricocheted off the dome, crashing into the others like a pinball.

"Now!"

At Fecanya's shout, the other fairies concentrated their magic into one big shove.

The imps were so distracted at being battered and bruised—and in some cases, knocked unconscious—by the ricocheting dancer, that they didn't know what hit them. Several managed to get their wits about them and pushed back.

"We can get them through," Fecanya yelled over the curses and screams of imps still being hit by the ricocheting breakdancer.

The three fairies groaned against the huge number of imps still struggling to break free.

From somewhere in the depths of Fecanya's extradimensional satchel, came the tune "Oh Yeah."

Sugressa glanced at her. "What's that? It sounds familiar."

Oooooh Yeah. Chicka chicka.

Fecanya glanced down at her satchel, then Sugressa. "It lets me know when my when my shift is over and the weekend starts."

They nearly faltered when a big lump of imps combined their efforts and pushed back.

"If we don't get them through now," Garbita groaned, "they'll break free. I don't have much left in me."

"Channel some of that hot air," Fecanya muttered.

"What?"

"One last push, together!"

Garbita narrowed her eyes, but nodded. The two fairies at Fecanya's sides gathered the last reserves of their energy and funneled their magic power into her. Fecanya nearly yelped at the sudden surge of power that filled her. She moved her hands about, molding the magic, spreading it. Finally, with a mighty, high-pitched grunt, she released a blast of magic that swept over the disgusting mass of evil Fae.

There was the sound of stumbling and falling as the pile of imps were shoved through the gateway, and tripped over the knuckle-dragger. "Oomph. Argh! Stop touching me! That's my ribs! Geroff me! My spine! Ung!"

Once the last of the things were through, Fecanya sealed the gateway by making a zipper motion, and snapping her fingers. Once she was sure it was done, she bent over and put her hands on her knees to catch her breath.

"That was ... rather ... stressful," Garbita panted. "I do hope ... Bloomara and those ... Abatwa managed to stop the flow. I don't have enough in me to stop a second attempt by those dreadful things."

"Um ... Fecanya?"

"What?" When no answer came, she looked over at Sugressa in irritation. "What?"

"Um ... I think you dropped something."

Fecanya looked at where the sugar fairy pointed, and felt her heart shrivel up to the size of a raisin. On the ground about half a foot from her feet, lay a long, slender wand covered in pink glitter with a big sparkling five-point star on the end of it. Pink dust puffed out of it as though the thing was breathing.

With a guilty glance at the other two fairies "normal" wands, Fecanya summoned as much dignity as she could salvage slowly, deliberately, bent down and picked up the wand. She opened her bag and dropped it in, hoping in vain that the thing would continue to fall forever and cease to exist.

"Was that your wand?"

"No."

"But it looked like ..."

"NO."

"Oh don't be like that, Fecanya," Sugressa said. "It's cute!"

Fecanya ground her teeth.

"That was quite a ... lovely, wand."

She heard the barely contained laughter in Garbita's voice and wanted to throttle the Garbage Fairy.

Out of Ordure

Chapter Twenty-one

It seemed inappropriate that no dust puffed into the air when Leowitriss dropped the tome that was Fecanya's file on his desk.

"Ahem-hem." He pushed his half-moon spectacles up the bridge of his nose, and produced a manila folder from his drawer. "Ahem hem."

"I don't mind waiting if you wanna go gargle that," Fecanya said.

The therapist glanced over his glasses at her, then returned to the folder. "I must say …"

"Must you?"

"… that I'm pleasantly surprised by this report, Miss Fecanya." He slid his spectacles to the tip of his nose as he read. "Fine display of courage and cooperation with team members. Selflessness in returning to duty in a crisis. Stunning display of magical ability and competency. Genuine concern for others." He looked up at her, and there was surprise in that blue eyed gaze. "It says that your efforts bought enough time for the other fairies to shut down the connecting facilities, and for Miss Bloomara's Abatwa team to effectively sabotage the computer system at the mega plant."

Fecanya suspected that was only part of it. Her tiny helpers had likely brought half the system down during her fight with the imps, which was probably why the evil Fae weren't any stronger and numerous than they were. If they could have continued drawing more conduit material from the other plants, that battle could have ended differently. Just thinking about it made her shiver.

"Well done, Miss Fecanya. You've made excellent progress. I'm proud of you."

The satyr's smile faded when Fecanya reached into her satchel and withdrew a sweet bark cigarette. She snapped her fingers in front of it, and it lit in a lovely purple glow. She took a long pull, and had to refrain from rolling her eyes up into her head. *Oh that's good.*

"Must you smoke that in here?" the therapist asked in a plaintive voice.

"Sorry, Leo. I can't even remember the last time I've had one. And it's not like this thing is one of those toxic self-destruct tubes humans smoke. This is sweet bark. It's harmless."

"It's still smoke. And in my office."

She inhaled another puff, and practically sighed upon exhaling. "Well I'm feeling pretty relaxed right now, so if you want me to put it out, consider yourself warned."

"Ahem. Moving on …"

Fecanya grinned.

"In light of this new report, I'm thinking we might be able to move our sessions to three days a week, instead of daily. What do you think about that?"

"I can live with that."

"Thank goodness."

Fecanya frowned through her purple cloud. "What's that?"

"Nothing. I'll send my comments to Deliah Harmass with a recommendation that we reduce your sessions. As long as you continue to make progress like this, I see no reason to reduce them further. Well done, Miss Fecanya."

Fecanya stuck the cigarette between her lips and stood. She leaned across the desk and pinched the satyr's cheeks. "Oh you. You're making me feel all fuzzy inside, Leo. Does this mean we're like friends, or something?"

"Miss Fe*canya*! This is unacceptable behavior. And here we just spoke of your positive progress."

Fecanya giggled, then choked on the purple smoke. "Relax, I'm just having a little fun. You really need to loosen that paisley tie of yours, Leo. It's strangling your sense of humor." She looked him up and down. "You know that tie doesn't match your shirt, right?" She twirled her finger. "Lavender plaid?"

"My fashion tastes are none of your concern."

She giggled. "You got it, Leo."

"Leo ... *witriss.*"

* * *

"How'd your session go?" Sugressa chirped when Fecanya exited the office.

Fecanya frowned. "Were you waiting out here for me?"

"Isn't that what friends do?"

"Friends?"

"Of course."

Fecanya shrugged. "I s'pose."

"So what are your plans now?" Sugressa practically bounced with excitement. "You gonna finish off that vacation you took before the mega plant thing?"

"I didn't realize I was on a vacation," Fecanya replied. "I was thinking of it more as a retirement."

Sugressa waved the notion away. "Don't be silly. You'd drive yourself crazy."

Fecanya weighed a life of magically processing diverse types of dung from all over the greater Garmin area, against a life of sand between her toes, frozen drinks with tiny umbrellas, and her silent iguana friend, Linda. "I'm sure I'll manage."

"No matter where you go, there'll be dung, Fecanya. You're the best at what you do, and we all appreciate it."

Fecanya turned a puzzled expression on the sugar fairy. "You talk like I'm some superhero who feels under-appreciated."

"You *are* a superhero. In my book, at least." She shrugged. "It's easy to be cheerful when you make things sweet for a living, like me. But your job is much tougher, and you're still an awesome person! I admire you."

Fecanya stared at her. "Do you even *know* me?"

"Yes. And I think you're awesome!"

She's been sampling too much of her product. "Well … that's, nice, Sugressa. Um. Thank you."

Sugressa bounced her shoulders, then lunged in and wrapped her in a tight hug. "We should get together with the others and have a girls' night out, or something. It'll be fun."

Fecanya waved her hands in a warding gesture. "Whoa, whoa. Let's not go overboard. I'm willing to hang out with you. Maybe grab an appletini after work. But let's not go doing group happy hours or anything. I don't think I could handle that."

"Okay."

Fecanya saw the frown creasing Sugressa's forehead. "What?"

"I have a question."

This better not be about my wand. "Which is?"

"What was that thing you did, to beat the imp? You shouted that funny word. *Riduwken*, or something."

Fecanya chuckled. "It's *Hadouken*. Have you never heard of it? It's only from the most popular video game in history."

"You know we don't use human technology, Fecanya."

"Much to your loss."

They reached the Rotunda. Dwarves, miner goblins, and gnomes were calmly breaking down the tunnel seals and clearing out the rubble. Only the debris strewn about the place indicated that there had been any emergency at all.

"So what are you going to do?" Sugressa asked.

Fecanya looked past the sugar fairy, toward the top of the Rotunda. Toward her empty pod. She made a subtle gesture with her hands, and snapped her fingers. A small gateway opened behind her, and she glanced over her shoulder at the sandy beach and palm trees. She stepped through the gateway and smiled at Sugressa.

"Have a margarita."

Out of Ordure

Out of Ordure

Out of Ordure

About the Author

Ramón Terrell is an actor and author who instantly fell in love with fantasy the day he opened R.A. Salvatore's *The Crystal Shard*. Years (and many devoured books) later he decided to put pen to paper for his first novel. After a bout with aching carpals, he decided to try the keyboard instead, and the words began to flow.

As an actor, he has appeared in the hit television shows *Supernatural*, *iZombie*, *Arrow*, and *Minority Report*, as well as the hit comedy web series *Single and Dating in Vancouver*. He also appears as one of Robin Hood's Merry Men in *Once Upon a Time*, as well as an Ark Guard on the hit TV show *The 100*.

When not writing, or acting on set, he enjoys reading, video games, hiking, and long walks with his wife around Stanley Park in Vancouver BC.

Connect with him at:
http://rjterrell.com/
Ramon Terrell-author/actor on Facebook
@RamonTerrell on Twitter
Ramon Terrell on Goodreads

Out of Ordure

Other Titles by Ramón Terrell

Tal Publishing
Unleashed:
Saga of Ruination, Book One

WordFire Press
Echoes of a Shattered Age:
Legend of Takashaniel, Volume One

Running from the Night:
Hunter's Moon, Book One

Hunter's Moon:
Hunter's Moon, Book Two

61548039R00083

Made in the USA
Lexington, KY
13 March 2017